# MARK OF THE BEAST

There was evil in the air at the séance that would transform their lives. Janice said she had not changed but there were signs Alan could not ignore. Like the strange mark on her hand, the naked wanderings in the moonlight, the blood stains on her clothes . . . And so Alan turned to the ex-priest Ruane, a man drained of self-respect, a drunkard, a reject — the only man who would listen. A man who knew the reality of the devil.

*Books by Brian Ball*
*in the Linford Mystery Library:*

DEATH OF A LOW HANDICAP MAN
MONTENEGRIN GOLD
THE VENOMOUS SERPENT
MALICE OF THE SOUL
DEATH ON THE DRIVING RANGE
DEVIL'S PEAK

BRIAN BALL

◆

# MARK OF THE BEAST

*Complete and Unabridged*

**LINFORD**
*Leicester*

First published in Great Britain

First Linford Edition
published 2009

British Library CIP Data

Ball, Brian, *1932* –
Mark of the beast
1. Horror tales.
2. Large type books.
I. Title
823.9'12–dc22

ISBN 978–1–84782–636–7

Published by
F. A. Thorpe (Publishing)
Anstey, Leicestershire

Set by Words & Graphics Ltd.
Anstey, Leicestershire
Printed and bound in Great Britain by
T. J. International Ltd., Padstow, Cornwall

This book is printed on acid-free paper

# 1

'Tell your husband to park at the front,' Mrs. Pierce said.

'Park there,' ordered Janice, so Alan eased the Rover into the kerb.

Mrs. Pierce said: 'Charlie will be pleased you've come along. Though he's not been too well himself. He said last week he'd got a cold, but I think it's flu.'

'Flu, Mrs. Pierce!' said Alan as he locked the doors of the Rover.

'Do call me Linda. Charlie always neglected himself,' Mrs. Pierce said. 'I was always telling him to wrap up. Any little infection goes straight to his chest. He sounded dreadful last week.'

She led the way to the white-painted building.

'But isn't he — ' Alan began in a whisper.

'Alan!' warned his wife.

'But I thought you told me she'd lost her husband, Jan. I thought he was dead!'

1

Mrs. Pierce waited for them on the step. Smiling, she said:

'But Charlie's not dead, dear! How could he send me messages every week?'

Alan hadn't wanted to come to the séance. There was a good TV programme that evening. But Janice had been insistent. Now he was stuck with a crank.

'Well?' asked Mrs. Pierce.

'I suppose — '

'They don't regard it as death,' said Janice.

'That's right, dear,' said Mrs. Pierce. 'It's just a matter of going over to the other side.'

'Ah,' said Alan. 'The other side.' He repressed the urge to laugh as he caught the expression on the women's faces. 'Is it time to go in?'

'Yes! We're late!' said Mrs. Pierce. 'Janice, I'm sure you'll get through, though I don't know about your husband.'

Janice smiled, and her whole being was transfigured. She was a tall, slim, very pale girl with a long white neck and a well-shaped body; there was nothing exceptional at all about her except that smile. Her chin was too pointed and her nose too narrow for beauty. She was plain until she smiled.

Alan saw the brilliant smile on his wife's face and knew it wasn't for him. Janice was smiling because she was excited at the prospect of hearing a dead man speak. A dead man with flu.

# 2

Janice wished she had brought her coat. She could feel the goose pimples rising on her arms as they entered the hall.

'Mrs. Worrall's waiting to start,' whispered Linda Pierce at her side. 'We're late.'

Janice looked around the hall. The walls were white, the roof high with old wooden beams. About twenty people were sitting on straight-backed chairs in a semi-circle at the far end of the hall. Many more chairs were empty, but the atmosphere was cosy. There was a little conversation amongst the congregation, women talking to their neighbours; Janice saw only three or four elderly men amongst them.

She and Alan were the object of some curiosity, so she kept her best smile in place whilst she checked that Alan was not fidgeting or talking inanely to cover his embarrassment. If he kept quiet all would be well.

She didn't know if she was pleased or not that she had accepted Mrs. Pierce's invitation. There was a certain excitement in the prospect of attending a séance, of course, but there was another side to it. Most of the people in the hall had a rather common appearance.

'See, Mrs. Worrall, I've brought my visitors!' called Linda Pierce in an ingratiating voice. 'I'm sorry we're late, but we had to wait whilst they got the car parked. You said it would be all right to bring them along?'

The Charnocks noticed the negress for the first time. She was sitting amongst the others, to the right of the semi-circle.

'Hello. Good evening,' said Janice firmly.

'You did say I could bring my friends,' reminded Linda Pierce. 'And I did ask my Charlie, Mrs. Worrall.'

'You're welcome,' said the woman. 'Come and sit down.'

Alan inspected her. He was not impressed. Mrs. Pierce might defer to her, but he could find nothing about her to suggest that she had unusual qualities. Janice seemed happy enough, however.

He let her do the talking.

'I'm very glad to meet you, Mrs. Worrall,' Janice was saying quietly. 'Linda's told me all about your power. It's a very wonderful thing.'

Mrs. Worrall smiled back at Janice's radiant face.

'Oh, it's a small thing, dear, a gift that could come to anyone. I try to use it for good.'

The women on the chairs made small noises of admiration and agreement whilst Mrs. Worrall's broad, good-humoured face split into a grin. She had good teeth. Good teeth, hair tinted blue, a firm, heavy body, large brown arms and the most hideous of yellow dresses reaching to her ankles. He looked up to avoid her smile and saw the beams in the roof. Woodworm, he guessed, noting their raddled appearance. And then he thought of Charlie Pierce in his grave. Was it possible that this woman in her terrible dress could bring the man to some semblance of life?

Janice dug him in the ribs. 'Sit down,' she ordered.

'Next to me,' said Mrs. Pierce. She whispered: 'We sing a hymn and then the messages start. Old Mr. Purbeck is first. He's worried about his Sadie.'

'Poor thing,' said Janice. She would have said more, but Mrs. Worrall had risen.

'Brothers and sisters, we welcome tonight two guests, Mr. and Mrs. Charnock, introduced by our dear friend Linda Pierce.' She waited until the small murmurs of greeting and welcome died down. 'Shall we sing our usual hymn, brothers and sisters, to prepare ourselves for the call to our dear ones?'

Alan Charnock suffered acutely. He stumbled as he got to his feet. Mrs. Worrall hit a true note to lead the singing, quite loud by local standards. Alan didn't know the words and tried to look as though he was singing. But he was so much off-key that two or three of the singers turned to look at him. By the time the hymn had finished, he was heartily sick of Janice's interest in psychic phenomena.

Janice felt herself trembling when the

three verses of the hymn were sung. She helped to move chairs, conscious of a growing sense of mystery as the brown-skinned Mrs. Worrall supervised the alignment of the circle. It had seemed something of a joke when Mrs. Pierce told her that her dead husband wouldn't mind if she were to come to the séance; then, when Janice heard about Mrs. Worrall's successes in summoning the dead, she had become interested. She felt tremors running through her body. It was a little scary.

'Quiet,' she whispered to Alan as he settled into his chair.

'Please join hands,' said Mrs. Worrall. 'I feel we shall have a good communication this evening. The skies are clear and the earth is full of good vibrations.'

Again there were murmurs of pleased anticipation from the congregation. Around the circle, they began to take one another's hands, until all were linked, with the exception of the Charnocks and the medium.

Mrs. Worrall glanced around the circle of attentive faces. 'Your friends should join too,' she told Mrs. Pierce.

'Oh, they haven't linked hands yet! Janice — Alan — you can't sit out. It isn't allowed. You're either in the circle or you have to leave.'

Mrs. Worrall's smile was encouraging. Janice began to respond to the good nature of the woman. 'Hold Linda's hand,' she ordered.

Alan obeyed. He took his wife's hand too, and she, in turn, held out her hand to a small, stout woman. For Alan, it was a further small embarrassment. He hadn't held hands in public since childhood, not even with Janice. He felt his palms sweating and he wished the meeting over.

For Janice, there was a different sensation. The small feelings of rather fearful excitement gave way to much deeper and more complex emotions. She would have found it difficult to describe how she felt, but it seemed to her that she was experiencing sensations that she had not encountered often in her life, and then only for a few moments.

'It's not easy — the darkness!'

The words ended suddenly with a piercing shriek. It was echoed by the outgoing breath of the congregation; women called out aloud now. They had caught the distress in the strange, unearthly voice. Janice found herself calling too, but she did not know what she was saying. Beside her, Alan gripped her hand reassuringly.

She responded gratefully.

'What's happening, Jan?' he whispered. 'What's the old girl doing? I swear it's not her voice! It can't be — Jan?'

'I don't know, Alan.'

Someone asked a question:

'Is it the guide? Mrs. Worrall, is it the guide who can tell me of Sadie? How's my little Sadie, Mrs. Worrall? Is the Golden Girl ready to tell me how my little Sadie is?'

'Hush, Mr. Purbeck!' a woman called. 'Mrs. Worrall's having trouble!'

Janice was spellbound. Her breathing was jerky and irregular; her heart still pounded, but she could make out what was taking place. Alan wanted to ask questions. She told him to wait.

The medium appeared to be unconscious, yet she sat more or less upright in the chair. Her head had fallen to one side. The eyebrows still twitched, and her lips worked spasmodically as if more words struggled for exit. Suddenly she spoke again:

'Oh, yes! Yes, I am here!' The voice was clear and young, certainly not that of an immigrant from the West Indies. It was a cultured voice, one that had known breeding and education.

'I can hear! I can stay but not for long! The — the — *darkness*!'

And then the words were distorted, the sounds jumbled so that a mixture of strange consonants straggled out of the medium's mouth.

'How's my Sadie?' called the old man impatiently.

The answer came at once, quite clear and in the voice of the young girl. There was no doubt or hesitation: 'Sadie? Sadie with the limp and the bushy tail? I can see her now. She is so happy. Sadie is well — Sadie sends a bark for her master!'

And a small, snapping barking came

from the medium.

Alan stifled a groan. He had listened to the frantic squeals of the women in the circle, and to the maunderings of the old negress. Now, he felt that the whole performance was on the level of farce.

It appeared that the people who attended the séance did so to get in touch with their deceased pets. Alan thought of the story he would have to tell at the office; a smile came to his face, yet he quickly erased it. Janice was taking it all seriously. He would have to be careful not to let her see how he felt. Mild interest with just a little skepticism, that was the attitude.

He murmured encouragingly to her. Mrs. Pierce told him to be quiet.

Alan decided to discuss mysticism with Janice when they got home. It wouldn't be a bad thing to let her see that the people around her had been taken in by a bit of clever voice-modulation. Mrs. Worrall was clearly a first-rate mimic. She'd done the Golden Girl bit quite well, though she had gone bronchitic at one stage. Those grunts and groans were not in keeping with the rest of the performance. It was too much that the only effective message should be from a dead dog. Alan allowed himself a moderate smile as he looked about the circle.

Janice saw the disbelieving smile. It was like Alan, of course, to remain aloof when matters beyond the immediate perception of the senses were before him. He had a man's cold, practical mind, disregarding what he couldn't touch or see or have confirmed in writing by a couple of experts. Janice found herself disliking him greatly. But the feeling lasted only for moments. What was passing before her was of far greater interest.

Mrs. Worrall was in a trance; she was unconscious, but it was an odd kind of unconsciousness. A spirit guide was talking through her dark lips. More men and women, encouraged by her success with the dead Sadie, began to question the medium.

'Can you tell me anything about my mother?' asked one fairly well dressed woman of about fifty. 'She passed over last week and we do miss her so!'

Mrs. Worrall's lips moved:

' — not so dark now and the shadow passes — much light, much sweet light! Who calls?'

'Me, Golden Girl!' cried out the woman who had asked about her mother. 'Me, Mrs. Wyatt! It's about my mother — tell her we send our love!'

Janice was so moved by the woman's sad cries that she wept. There was no darkness, no feeling of danger, no hints of blackness and the deep caverns of the seas. The congregation assembled in the small Spiritualist church were her friends, and the lady who rolled and twitched and writhed in her straight-backed chair was the means through which the living around her contacted the dear departed. The momentary fear was past. The dead girl who was the spirit guide would help them.

Mrs. Worrall's lips moved easily, with no reluctance at all:

' — there is one near me,' came the voice of the cultured young woman, ' — faint voice, a new voice in this happy place of everlasting light — speak, speak to her — tell her who calls!'

Alan could hardly bear it. No doubt the medium would ask the congregation to take a collection when she had done with her wiles. Janice would probably contribute lavishly. The poor girl looked completely under the spell of the ridiculous negress. And the others too were deluded: take the woman who was trying to speak to her mother, dead only the week before. She was bending forward as though she was speaking into some kind of celestial telephone. Absurd!

'It's me, Mother!' she cried. 'Me, Ada!'

'*Ada!*' mouthed Alan silently. Good God!

A thin, tired, faraway sound came from the negress's lips:

' — tell her not to worry — tell Ada I can rest now. Tell Ada there's good luck coming.' The voice became stronger. 'Tell Ada I've left my cameo brooch in the teapot — tell her!'

As the voice faded and sank away, the men and women gasped in amazed delight. Janice was rather annoyed. It seemed to her that the powers of Mrs. Worrall should not be debased in this way: the women thought it a splendid prize.

Without thinking at all about what she was doing, she called out clearly and sharply:

'May I say something to the spirit guide? May I, Mrs. Worrall?'

Linda Pierce was both astounded and annoyed:

'I was next, Janice! I wanted to ask about my Charlie! He's been ill and — '

'*Oh!*' screamed the medium in the girl's clear voice. 'The dark! No more — darkness and danger! Oh, Golden Girl fears the shadows!'

Abruptly the atmosphere changed. Where there had been a mild, pleasurable feeling of self-congratulation, there was doubt. The fear returned.

No one moved. No one uttered a sound.

The last of the light was gone. The skylights were patches of grey, the walls dark, and closer than before.

All attention was on the medium. Mrs. Worrall's whole body shook in the chair.

Her heels drummed three, four times on the old wooden floor. Strange guttural noises came from deep within her chest. The congregation sat rigid, hands biting into one another, the circle unbroken and every eye on the medium in her eerie delirium.

'Shadows! Danger — darkness!' yelled the medium. 'Golden Girl afraid of the dark — afraid of the life-that-is-not-life, fears the life-that-is-not-life!'

'Is she all right?' whispered Alan. 'What's she talking about? What's happening, Mrs. Pierce?'

In the deep silence the medium's strange voice again called out; this time it was a hopeless, wailing cry:

' — can't help now, the thing-that-never-was-life is too strong — can't keep it away from dear life-that-is-your-life — danger!'

'I've had enough,' said Alan. He tried to release his hands. He had large, strong hands, yet he could not break free. And then he did not wish to, for something that defied all reason took shape in the gloom.

About the head of the medium, a thin, insubstantial grey-white shape was forming, weirdly, from spinning white and grey motes like black sunshine.

'Jan, let's go,' whispered Alan. 'Help me, Jan!'

Janice smiled her most brilliant smile.

'Whatever for, darling? The fun's only just beginning.'

# 3

Alan Charnock was an educated man, who, by virtue of his professional training, had the ability to observe and then describe what he saw. Later he was to attempt to recall what his senses impressed on his mind; it was to prove difficult. He could remember his wife's calm voice: he had no trouble in recapturing the initial stunned horror of the congregation; but what caused their horror — and his own — was a thing of such insubstantial appearance that it was to defy a complete analysis.

A shape seemed to hover behind the medium, a rearing, upright figure. There was the suggestion of a shape — no features, yet unquestionably a head and a torso. It was as though a large shadow had been cast which then took on a third dimension, solidity. There was a body and a head. Even the features were there somewhere. Within the mistiness of the shape, they lay as in a rough-hewn block of stone. There was menace too.

Alan knew that something had gone terribly wrong with the séance. Calling on a spirit guide was part and parcel of the business of Spiritualism. The simple folk in the hall had made the kind of request he had expected them to make, small enquiries about someone they had loved and who had died. It had been rather a joke that the enquiries should extend to the state of health of a dead pet, but the comic side of it had passed.

A grim and evil thing was taking shape before the frightened congregation.

Mrs. Worrall's lips moved again. Alan could see bright drops of blood on the medium's chin. Sounds grated in her throat.

It was not the cultured tones of the spirit guide, nor did the sounds appear especially human. They were much worse than the noises that Alan had taken to be a rather poor effort at projecting a mystical voice. A harsh, croaking issued from the bitten lips, a jangling wild sound that rang round Alan Charnock's head with a vicious insidiousness.

As the words spewed out a penetrating and vile odour filled the immediate area around the medium. Alan felt his gorge rising as the stench of outlandish and poisonous fumes crept to his nostrils. Unbelieving, yet unable to deny the validity of what was happening, Alan Charnock knew that the stench came from the grotesque, misty shape. And that the guttural sounds emanated from it too, for no longer did the medium's lips move. She slumped in her chair without movement.

On either side of her, the middle-aged women who had supported her when she had first gone into her trance were themselves dazed and nerveless. Yet the hands held, as if fused together. No matter the horror they were experiencing — and Alan knew they saw as he did — they were quite incapable of freeing themselves from the grip of their neighbours in the dreadful circle.

No one could move.

It was at the moment of heart-stopping terror that Alan Charnock turned to

Janice. When he saw the shining eyes the great wide smile, the rise and fall of bosom, and the sheer joy in her face, he panicked.

'Janice, Jan?' he said aloud. 'Janice, let's go, darling — please? Christ, Jan, what's wrong!'

Janice's eyes were like jewels. She did not see him. She did not hear his words. The ghastly apparition had altogether entranced her.

'Jan!'

Her lips moved as slowly and agonizingly as Mrs. Worrall's:

'Keli — Kelipoth — Kelipoth? I hear, I hear!'

'Christ, Jan — '

As he spoke, Alan felt the hands in his become convulsively alive. A rippling, surging current passed through his palms, first from the right hand, then from the left. Backwards and forwards it raced, and all the time, the thing behind Mrs. Worrall raised itself to the dark skylights, snuffling, seeking, smelling out the soul that might respond to its call.

Alan Charnock's senses reeled.

He caught a glimpse of Jan's face again. She was radiant He saw the insubstantial beast looming larger and larger in the darkness of the hall. He retched as the rottenness of the pit assailed him. He found himself sinking forward towards the floor, and still the hands on either side of him bit deep the fierce current shooting through and through his body, its source the hands.

Minutes passed like this, in a half-state between unconsciousness and a waking dream. Shapes merged, figures writhed, horrific sounds came to his ears; and not all of it registered on his battered mind. He knew there was more, that strange and weird events were taking place around him, just beyond the edges of what had seemed a normal world.

And then it was over.

He blinked and it was gone.

'Wake up,' he heard Janice saying. 'Alan. You've let me down again! Oh, look at him, Linda, he's dozed off.'

Alan Charnock blinked again. He raised his hands to rub his eyes.

'Dozed off? Have I, Jan? Then what about — '

He stopped. Self-control reasserted itself. He would not make a fool of himself. He looked at Janice, at Linda Pierce, and around the circle; and then, fearfully towards Mrs Worrall. The medium was hidden from his view.

To gain time, he apologized. 'I'm sorry, Jan. You know me. I've not felt too well.' He attempted a laugh, though to his own ears it sounded hysterical. 'I must have — well, I thought — '

Janice stared at him with no affection in her gaze. 'What?'

Alan Charnock floundered. His eyes darted about the hall. No one seemed to be unduly alarmed. There was no hint of the strange terror that had gripped the Spiritualists. Mrs. Pierce sat calmly, her hands in her lap. The stout woman was perspiring a little, though she had done so from the moment she sat down. Why, when they had been so profoundly disturbed by the monstrous apparition, did they now seem so calm? It couldn't be that the thing was expected was a commonplace visitation? And Mrs. Worrall — what of her? The women still hid her from his view.

He shuddered and looked down at his trembling hands. *A dream? He had been asleep?*

'What, Alan?' repeated Janice.

Alan Charnock kept a tremor from his voice: 'It was the — I saw the — ' He couldn't go on.

'Alan!'

'But I heard it — The message!'

It wasn't what he meant to say. He wanted to tell her that the thing had grunted and snarled, that it stank of substances he could no longer put a name to; and especially that the others had seen it too.

'I don't see how you could have heard much,' said Janice. 'You dropped off when it was getting interesting.'

'Getting interesting — that's what you said, Jan! Don't you remember — you said something like 'The fun's just starting'?'

Janice sighed and got to her feet.

'Linda, don't pay any attention to him.

I think he might be sickening for something.'

Linda Pierce got up too.

'It's a pity my Charlie didn't get through. I'll have to ask him about his chest next week.'

Alan began to believe that he had fallen asleep. There was no sign that the terrible apparition had affected anyone else. Small groups of women chatted to one another. Someone had turned on the lights, and the hall no longer had the tomb-like atmosphere of so short a time before

But what about Mrs. Worrall? Alan nervously scrambled to his feet, and took a few steps towards the knot of women about the medium. Surely she at least must show some evidence of the thing that had used her as a channel from God knew what other world? Even as he caught sight of Mrs. Worrall's kindly smiling face. Alan started to explain everything away.

She was grey-brown rather than the muddy coffee colour she had been; yet her white smile was firmly in place. Her lips were slightly ragged in two places, yet she appeared to suffer no distress on that account. There was no blood. And she was listening to the admiring congratulations of her small circle of devotees with every sign of enjoyment

Alan remembered the grunting, the half-formed sounds of incantation that might have been the language of a savage. A dream? It had to be a dream. Janice was looking at him with less distaste now. He shook his head.

'I'm sorry, Janice,' he said again. 'It sounds crazy, but I've had some kind of hallucination. I suppose the atmosphere and everything did it — I thought Mrs. Worrall had a sort of fit, and that we all saw a sort of — '

'Sort of what, Mr. Charnock,' asked Linda Pierce.

'Well, I thought I saw a bloody ghost!'

'We don't talk about such things!' Linda Pierce told him frostily. 'The dear departed are not to be mixed up with that sort of talk!'

It was with a sense of relief that Alan Charnock heard his wife apologizing to the nearest of the Spiritualists. She was invited to return on another occasion, but the offer pointedly excluded him; he felt wretched, humiliated and yet troubled. A small remnant of masculine pride made him insist on driving to a pub on the outskirts of the small town.

'Where do you think you're going, Alan?' asked Janice.

'I felt like a drink.'

'You don't drink.'

'I feel like one now — I feel a bit shattered.'

'You'll feel worse in the morning.'

'Jan, I just want one drink, that's all! I didn't feel too well at the séance.'

Alan saw his wife's pale face set in harsh lines, so that it was in a state of some melancholy that he escorted Janice into the Lounge Bar of the 'Coach and Horses'.

'A large brandy,' he told the landlord. 'And a sweet sherry for my wife.'

# 4

Janice Charnock felt drowsy. She was annoyed with her husband, but not as much as he thought. The evening had excited her, though she would not admit as much to Alan. It didn't do to let men know what you thought. They knew too much already.

She cast her mind back to the events of the seance.

Linda Pierce had promised a strange kind of communication — it seemed somehow thrilling and stimulating to hold a conversation with a person who had died. Charlie Pierce. He had been in his grave for years; and yet Linda believed that she could talk to him as if he was a customer in the shop. Alan was not impressed, of course.

His scorn at the questions of that old fool who had wanted to have his dog bark back at him was only too apparent. If she hadn't felt so excited — so *odd* — Janice could have laughed. Alan wouldn't have liked that. But there had been the other feeling.

Janice clenched her hands secretly into her thighs. She was sure that the skin on her palms was broken. It was a frightening experience, that sudden jolt of burning and yet soothing force that had flowed through and through her. She didn't want to feel it again. Once was enough.

She cleared her throat. Alan was annoyed with her. He had finished one brandy — a double — and if she didn't conciliate him a little he would drink more. She said:

'Alan, what on earth's bothering you? You're morbid tonight. Let's go. I'm tired.' To reinforce her point, she added: 'I've got a headache.'

'You can have an aspirin when we get back.'

Alan Charnock's confusion of mind had resolved itself to some extent. He knew he would be sick in the morning. It didn't seem to matter. A duodenal ulcer, the doctor had said. Don't drink, don't smoke, bed early, avoid excitement, take exercise in moderation and drink plenty of milk. All this Alan had done for a year, and yet the ulcer rode in his guts. It was time to counter-attack.

Tonight, he would get drunk.

He smiled at the landlord, a large and uncouth man who did not notice his attempt at friendliness. An old drunk with a broad red face stared at the rows of bottles. Alan asked for brandy.

'And a sherry?' asked the landlord.

'No. She's had enough.'

The landlord nodded uninterestedly. The drunk fumbled with his whisky glass. Alan raised his own glass as the man gulped down the whisky. He felt almost lightheaded. Memories tumbled through his brain, unpleasant memories, leftovers from the strange hallucinatory experience in the dingy hall. He blotted them out. The pub was warm and comfortable.

Alan watched as the man pursued an erratic course amongst the tables. He would pass near Janice. And Alan knew the man would stumble even as he did so. Janice was sipping her sherry as he pitched against her. It was a complete accident — he tried to grasp a chair-back, missed, and knocked Janice's glass out of her hand. Janice did not say a thing.

Janice's hand was still outstretched, so that they formed a tableau, she with golden wine soaking into the flowers of the dress; the drunk mumbling stupidly as he got to his feet.

'I'm sorry — ' the drunk began to apologize. He stared at her hand.

He would have said more, but Janice's cold smile stopped him. He looked into her face and shuddered. Then he turned away. She watched him as he stumbled out of the Lounge Bar.

It was the second time that Alan had experienced fear that evening.

Once during that odd dream or hallucination or whatever it was — and this was the second time. It was Janice's look of icy, implacable hostility that frightened him now. The landlord followed him to the table.

'Sorry about that, sir,' said the landlord. 'Can we get you a cloth or something, Missus?' he asked Janice

'It's quite all right.'

'Get the lady another drink, shall I?'

'No,' said Janice. 'I've had enough.'

'He was drunk,' said Alan. 'It was just bad luck. I'm sorry I brought you.' He reached for her hand and saw the red mark on the palm. 'Have you hurt yourself, Jan?'

She took her hand away, but not before he had seen the bright red mark.

'It's nothing. A rash. I must be allergic to something.'

Ideas tumbled through Alan's mind. The right hand, the hand that had held his left: it was marked, clearly marked, with an imprint that was as red as the berries of belladonna.

'You have hurt it, Jan. Let me see.'

Janice stood up. 'No, Alan. I want to go home. It's nothing. A rash. Something I've eaten. It doesn't matter.'

'It does!'

Janice's whole attitude changed. The challenge and the harshness went out of her face as if someone had erased it — wiped it clean and left it open and smiling.

'See, love, it's only a bit of a rash. I think it might be eating strawberries. We had some in the shop today.'

The bad moment passed.

When they were getting into the Rover, Alan sensed the presence of a figure in a shop doorway. He looked round and saw the heavy, stooped figure of the drunk. Alan couldn't see his face in the gloom, but he could make out the way the shoulders hunched forward and the head pointed towards the car. Fortunately Janice didn't see him. It had been an odd kind of evening. Alan was glad it was over.

# 5

Ruane waited for sleep. If he was lucky, it would come soon. He reached for the bottle and remembered it was empty. No whisky; tonight, no sleep. If it was another bad night, the old landlady would throw him out. Already she was suspicious.

She hadn't believed he was an out-of-work brickie. One look at his hands had been enough. He looked down at them. Useless soft hands — large enough, but with no skill. Trembling now because the nerve-endings needed the deadening effect of alcohol.

Ruane shook his head:

'You're the fool, Ruane,' he said aloud.

He put his hands behind his head. Soon he would have to come to terms with absolute destitution and learn its harsh lessons. Where to get a handout. Where to sleep. He thought of the Midlands parish he had once served; the sick teenagers had found a couple of meths drinkers and set light to them. Ruane traced a crack in the limed ceiling and wished for oblivion.

He was still watching when a thin wavering band of moonlight began to grow so that the flowers on the peeling wallpaper became great white cauliflowers. Ruane pushed aside the two thin blankets and stumbled to the window.

The terraced house was set high on the north side of the small coal and wool town. Ruane could see clear across the nineteenth-century tenements to the mills; beyond them, the winding gear of the old colliery. At either side of the town, the yellow lights picked out the path of suburban development, house after house neatly set in a small and well-fenced plot.

His hands shook on the cold window-frame. No skills in his hands, no will to find a job, no wish to live, no especial urge to die. He knew his shambling gait frightened young children.

Ruane stood for more than an hour by the window. It gave him an odd satisfaction to feel the night's cold seeping into his bones. He almost fell asleep.

The flaring pain, when it hit him, sent him reeling back into the bedroom, arms outflung and legs buckling, head bright with agony. He knew he yelled, but not what he called out.

Sound echoed inside his skull. One sound, a great malicious yell, something from the far side of the grave, a triumphant, bawling, mocking, slavering sound. By the time its echoes ceased in Ruane's large head, he heard other sounds.

'What do you think you're at! In my house, at dead of night — waking the neighbours — drunk and raving like Barney's pig? You're drunk! So give it up, or you'll be out on the street!'

Ruane opened his eyes and made out the woman's scrawny shape against the unshaded lamp. She said it all again. And again.

He heard. *Drunk?* Surely not? He counted the drinks again — four. Five. Maybe another. Say six. Then two pints of beer. That wasn't enough to be drunk on.

It didn't begin to bend the mind's shadows back.

Ruane got to his feet. The woman yelled at him again. He pushed past her. He had been standing at the window when the pain jolted him back like a great blast of gunfire.

'The window frame,' he mumbled. 'It swung and hit me.'

He knew it hadn't.

The pain had come from outside, a vicious and grotesque force that burst upon him because he was standing just here . . . It came from . . .

Ruane looked out over the sleeping town. Street lights. Late cars, beams flashing. A church tower. Not high, not impressive, he noted with a professional detachment. Mills. In the moonlight, stark and still, the winding gear of the former colliery. The workers' houses. Other houses. Boxes, row upon row. Small trees in the gardens, large fences round each box. There, thought Ruane. *There* . . .

This time the pain was unbearable. It ground his brain into mind-blasting agony. The nervous system collapsed.

Twenty minutes later, Ruane came to his senses. He could still hear the grotesque, swelling, vicious noise inside his head. There was a message, uncontrolled and vindictive, but not particularly for him, Ruane. It was for anyone who could recognize the challenge.

'God help me,' whispered Ruane.

He slowly made the sign of the Cross.

★ ★ ★

When they reached the house, Alan Charnock made the usual nightcap, a pot of milky drinking chocolate. It was his chore. Janice would look through a magazine or watch the tail end of the telly programmes. He turned on the electric fire beside the bed and draped Janice's black nightdress before it. She appreciated small, thoughtful gestures like that. Hot chocolate, a little chat and then sleep. Janice was likely too upset for anything else. The curtains hadn't been drawn.

He glanced out at the moonlit garden. The close cut grass shimmered in parallel bands. Alan had already begun to pull on the curtain cord when he saw the slim white shape in the glaring moonlight.

'Jan!' he said aloud.

She couldn't hear, of course, not through the double-glazing. Alan's immediate reaction was to open the window and call down to her. He stopped the movement of his hands towards the window-catch.

Maybe Janice had some perfectly good reason for standing there in the chill of the evening. But *naked?*

Her long blonde hair was halfway down her back. Her hands lay at her sides, her body quite upright. There was no motion in her body. She might have been a statue placed there a hundred years ago. Alan had the curious impression she had no intention of moving.

Only two or three minutes passed like this. For Alan Charnock, it seemed longer. Dimly he felt anger but it was a raging calm in his mind, not an anger that was likely to result in action. Resentment followed. The neighbours would see, of course, and there would be talk.

Even a mild sensation could imperil his career; a wayward wife was the last thing you wanted if you had only the vague promise of a partnership. Wives with wakeful infants would look across the backs of the gardens and see Janice. *Kinky* would be the verdict. Kinky Jan Charnock, her with the handsome husband. There was rarely anything of interest to discuss over the morning coffee.

Alan had worked himself up into a quiet rage and was about to open the window and hiss sharply to Janice when he detected another shape in the garden. It writhed in the sharp moonlight, a squat and flattened shape.

'It's a dog,' he thought, recognizing the thing. 'It's the Baines-Ogdens' dog.'

Alan could laugh at the momentary trickle of fear. The dog, not much more than a pup, some sort of wire-haired terrier, had got into their garden and was begging for food. It had seen Jan. And, dog-like, it was crawling on its belly to show it knew it shouldn't be there.

Janice didn't move. The dog moved

near and now Alan saw that its eyes looked ahead with a curiously blank expression, unblinking and huge. It's belly left a trail on the striped carpet of lawn.

Alan remembered that Janice detested dogs. Cats she revered, large Persians for preference. Dogs were noisy, they stank, they clawed and fawned; so why should Janice wait . . .

Her right hand moved slightly. Something gleamed. Metal. The dog rolled over, belly up. Alan heard himself saying, '*I don't think you ought to, Jan*,' when she turned to look up at him.

She was smiling. Just like the smile in the dingy hall. It unnerved him. Fingers trembling, he opened the window and saw that the dog had not moved.

'Jan, hadn't you better come in? It's cold, love.' He wanted to say that it wasn't his fault that she was interrupted, but he couldn't say it, for it admitted far too much of what he might be able to guess about her reason for standing so long, naked, blade ready, the animal crawling towards her in stark terror. Oh no. Say nothing, because nothing had happened. Nothing *could* have happened.

The bloody dog was after a cat. Janice had called it. Frightened, it had tried to make its peace by belly-crawling to her.

She moved out of his vision like a wraith. The dog rolled over onto its side and lay quietly for a minute.

Then it put its head back, howled once and raced for the gap in the hawthorns at the back of the house. Alan Charnock walked downstairs quietly and took the drinks tray into the lounge.

Janice was waiting.

'Christ,' whispered her husband. He slopped most of the hot chocolate onto the tray. Janice didn't seem to notice.

She was half-lying, half-sitting, on the most expensive piece of furniture the Charnock's possessed, a ten-foot divan-settee. Its dusky pink fibres shone with a delicate lustre in the dimly-lit room. Janice's skin reflected the faint glow.

'I've spilled the chocolate,' he said.

It didn't look like Janice. Janice never *posed*.

His heart smashed inside his chest like

a steam-hammer.

He had seen images like this on posters for films, on the covers of lurid paperback novels. They were large-bosomed, lewd, bold-eyed women, who anyway posed like that only for the delectation of a minority of men who couldn't take their pleasures normally and within the confines of a happy marriage.

Janice sleeked her blonde hair back.

'Come here.'

'Janice, we'll be seen! The curtains — '

'Here.'

The mugs clattered.

'Jan, don't you want the chocolate?'

She told him what to do with the chocolate — graphically.

He had never heard her use such words before. Not once. 'Pardon?'

'*Come here!*'

'I thought you were mad at me.'

'Me, sweetie?' It didn't seem possible that his wife could be so erotic.

'Jan, we don't, not here — not on the settee!' As her hand reached his neck, he experienced such a blast of furious lust that he could not control his breathing.

Janice had never looked like this or talked like this before. He struggled wildly for balance on the smooth artificial fur.

'For God's sake, let me breathe! Jan, we'll be seen! The Bentleys — the neighbours — they can see in — Jan!'

She bit his ear.

'Jan, don't bite! Jan, the curtains!'

She enveloped him with a shaking, surging movement, teeth snapping, eyes glazed in the pinkness of her pale face, fingers plucking at his hair . . .

★   ★   ★

Two miles away, Ruane tried to answer the old woman's fears. She wanted to know if he got moonstruck in drink. It was meant in the simple, country way: was he affected by the phases of the moon?

'It's the migraine, you must have heard of it,' he told her. 'Headaches, that's what it is, Mrs. Briggs.'

She wanted to bring him tea, for she could sense his loneliness and fear. It was a bizarre coincidence that she should then ask if his headaches had anything to do with his work.

'Dear God, I hope not,' he said, knowing he was wrong. 'I hope to God it hasn't.'

When she was gone, he lay back on the hard mattress, and curiously, sleep was not long in coming. The shock had exhausted him, he guessed. It would serve where the booze had failed. He drifted into grim dreams, almost surfacing to wakefulness a number of times.

There had been the unmistakable reek of evil over the town, an ancient and powerful evil. *Imaginings*, Ruane tried to tell himself when he was near waking. Half-drunken imaginings. Which anyway were not the concern of a priest the Church had dismissed. Let those whose duty it was to fight them take on the devils. He had his own to contend with.

Ruane slept.

# 6

Alan dressed hastily. It was seven-thirty, early for him to be up and about; but he had slept badly and he wished to avoid his wife's morning display of irritation. Janice wasn't a morning person, never had been. He hurried over his breakfast. There were too many questions he would have to ask her if he waited for Janice to get up.

Very quietly he said to her shallow-breathing form:

'I've got a couple of early calls, Jan. Get the bus, will you? 'Bye, love.'

An hour later Janice awoke and hoped it would all retreat from her memory.

'I must have been drunk!' she sobbed into her pillow. 'It's his fault. He gave me all that sherry to drink!' She raised herself up, glad of a familiar sense of annoyance. 'Alan!' she called.

She caught sight of her fingers. She opened her right palm, shuddering at what she knew would be there.

The mark glowed under the stains.

'Alan!' she bawled.

There was a darkness inside her head now. Waves of darkness flooded through her mind. It was as if she swam into thick, salty waters where lost creatures swayed in the depths and where she alone was alive. She ran downstairs and scrubbed at the mark with the most powerful detergent she could find. The skin began to shred. She tried undiluted bleach until the pain doubled her up.

'I should wash my mouth out too!' she grated at her reflection in the kitchen mirror. 'Dirty-minded cow! Dirty words! Why did you say them — *why*! You should be whipped! And in the garden — '

'Only me!' called Myra Bentley.

'Myra, make me a cup of tea, I'm late for work.'

'Wasn't Alan in a hurry this morning. He's out and about early.'

*Had the prying bitch seen?* Turning, Janice looked into the china-blue eyes. With women like Myra you couldn't always tell.

'How did the séance go?'

'Not bad. I've got to rush.'

'Let me see that hand!'

Janice snatched it away from the cup. 'It's just a rash! It's nothing.'

'Looks nasty.'

Janice found the opening. 'We were up late. I thought you might have heard us rowing,' Janice lied.

She waited anxiously. Myra said:

'I took a pill and went early.'

So she had been asleep. Janice allowed the long sigh of relief to escape slowly.

'I was a bit of a bitch to Alan. Things have got on top of me just lately.'

'That hand is nasty.'

'I'll miss my bus if I don't rush.'

'You've plenty of time for the half-past.'

The palm itched and hurt. It needed some kind of soothing ointment. There was a good selection on the shelves. As she walked to the bus stop, Janice began to concoct a story for Alan to explain her behaviour of the previous night; if she didn't, he'd expect the same kind of treatment every night, and that wasn't what marriage was for.

'Janice!' called her other next-door neighbour as she ran. 'Janice, stop Andrew!'

The two-year-old child had a good start, but Janice had been a runner at school. The fresh air and the morning sunshine brought a flood of vigour and pleasure through her young muscles. She looked into the distance and saw that there were several people at the bus stop; plenty of time to catch Andrew.

Laughing, she bent to scoop the squealing, red-faced infant. Her hand brushed his back.

The child shrieked and Janice's mind thundered with tormented images. For a moment she saw the terrier's eyes, wide and round, and then the dog's eyes were this screaming infant's, and a choking, searing pleasure screamed through her mind.

'Andy, oh poor Andy!' called Claire Baines-Ogden. 'What did you do to him, Janice?'

Large and square, the woman tried to stop her. The infant wailed at their feet. Janice looked down at the bright raw mark on her palm.

Claire Baines-Ogden heaved her son up. He began to beat her head, still screaming.

'*Andy!*'

Janice ran for the bus. She found herself wishing the woman dead. A darkness full of confused images of violence hung over her thoughts on the journey into the centre of Mersey Pagnall. She welcomed it, as a night traveller welcomes the distant lights of a village. The shapes in the gentle and comforting darkness became clearer. By the time she reached the shop, the palm had stopped itching.

Janice knew the skin was whole again. A curious calm came over her.

What did it matter? *I've done things I wouldn't tell anyone about*, she told herself, though this wasn't right, for if you had chosen to do them why should you feel ashamed? Anyway what was wrong with sex? What was wrong with standing in the moonlight watching the terrier crawl towards you and listening to its whimperings and knowing that soon it would roll just as you commanded, *just as the life-that-must-have-life commands*, the thing at the edges of her mind whispered until the whispering grew to a shout, then a great shapeless howling!

★ ★ ★

Janice moved about like an automaton all morning until the mindless fury wrenched her into blackness, so that she slid from the till and sent the display of razor blades and chocolate scattering over the few morning customers, bringing mingled annoyance and concern; and Linda Pierce to hold her forward so that the blood came back to her head and she could try to obey. *Obey!*

'Janice, what's wrong! You've gone as white as a sheet — you've grazed your head — it's bleeding. Oh where's that useless manager! Get her some water!' she called to a frightened young assistant who was nevertheless glad to have the tedium of the day relieved.

The manager came, a dapper bald little man.

'She'll have to go home,' he pro-
nounced. 'I'm sorry about this,' he told
the customers. 'Put a tissue to that cut,
Mrs. Pierce.'

Janice felt herself swimming in the
darkness, though nothing was clear about
her. Nothing was what it seemed. Calling
Alan things like — like what she
had called him, though it had seemed
funny at the time — and standing in the
garden, without clothes. *Why?* It was so
stupid!

'Hold this,' ordered Mrs. Pierce.

Janice took the tissue and pressed it
against her head. She stared as the older
woman supervised the tidying up of the
fallen displays. The tissue fell away, and
Janice saw the brilliant scarlet of fresh
blood.

'You've to go home,' said Linda Pierce
briskly. 'You'd better go to bed.'

Janice nodded. It was so confusing. You
glimpsed an idea of what to do, but the
faint thread of understanding snapped
almost at once.

'I'll take her in the car,' said the
manager reluctantly.

But Janice had seen Linda Pierce staring at the mark on her hand. 'Thanks, but I'll be all right now. I'll go on the bus.'

'What's that on your hand?'

'Nothing.'

There was a dim awareness in the woman's lined face. Their eyes met and Janice could feel the power within her surging and locking onto the older woman's will; Linda Pierce shivered. Before she could speak again, Janice said:

'Where does she live?'

'Who?'

'You know!'

'No.'

She knew now.

'Where?' said Janice, smiling.

'Why do you want her?'

'You'd better tell me.'

'I wish I'd never taken you! I thought you'd be receptive, but you're not, you're full of — '

'What?'

Linda Pierce could not take up the challenge in the thin white face. Hypnotized by that chilling smile, she bit back the sharp words that sprang to her lips.

'So where does the old cow live?' smiled Janice.

★   ★   ★

Alan Charnock was attempting to convince himself that there was a rational explanation for the evening's apparently strange happenings.

'Interesting sort of evening,' he said to one of the junior partners at Tomlinson & Hood's. 'Thought we'd go into this spiritualist business — you know, messages from the grave. 'Are you receiving me, Auntie Flo,' and all that.'

'Was she?'

Alan could only think of the terrible dreamlike trance. Involuntarily he shuddered.

'No! But there was something, Jerry. Weird as it sounds, it worked.'

Jerry Hood looked up from his desk. He was a small, ugly man of about thirty. He was mildly intrigued.

'Where was this?'

Alan set the scene. The medium, the questions to the spirit guide, and the eerie dream.

'So you fell asleep.'

'Funny thing,' agreed Alan, who didn't think so.

'Going again?'

'No!'

'How did the wife like it?'

'It turned her on!'

Jerry's brown face was still for moments. Then it cracked into a smile and Alan endured the humiliation of ribald laughter.

'Janice! *Janice!* No!'

Alan bit his lip. Then Jerry croaked:

'Well, what was it like, man? Christ, Alan, *what was it like*?'

Alan remembered Janice's smile.

He copied it.

'You dog,' said Jerry, and a flicker of pride revived in Alan's tormented soul. Jerry leant over and poked Alan in the belly. 'Well, it takes some nerve, it really does — Christ, wait till I tell them at the Round Table!'

'It was a bit odd, though,' Alan said

when Jerry stopped cackling. 'The meeting, I mean. I got this feeling that there really was something in it. I got a bit worked up when I thought I saw a ghost or when I dreamt I did.'

'Ectoplasm,' said Jerry. 'My old grannie used to go in for it. They do it with sprays nowadays. A puff or two of the old aerosol and there's your ghost.'

'It was more of a — '

Jerry knew everything.

'Creepy music. Touch of table-tapping from the clockwork hammers. Electronic crystal balls — they make them in Formosa. Ghosts with crystal balls — oh, mate!'

'Jan got a bit worked up,' said Alan, trying to break into the flow.

'I must take my missus. Or have a go at home. I could get the lot from a trick shop. They all stock the stuff. I might just do that next time I'm in Manchester. It was all on the telly early this year — didn't you see the programme?'

'No, it was Jan's friend's idea — '

'She's got a friend?'

'She's old.'

'Pity.'

Alan wanted to ask about wifely behaviour, but Jerry was already looking at a valuation, and the only sign that the conversation had taken place was a fading glimmer of amusement on his brown face.

Alan Charnock began to feel more relaxed. Maybe Jerry Hood had the right of it about the Spiritualists. The medium was a clever trickster. Perhaps she had some ability to induce a mood of fear in a receptive audience. Some of its members might easily become hypnotized if they were tired or weak-willed. *Like me*, Alan decided. *Asleep and dreaming.* The same with Jan. She had drunk a glass of sherry. She had been over-tired and therefore suggestible too. And it had been a fantastic bit of loving.

Jan would laugh about it. He began to wish he had discussed it with her the night before. It hadn't been a knife. No. There was a simple explanation for everything that had happened.

Feeling pleasantly relaxed, Alan called in to see Janice after his customary

58

sandwich at half-past twelve. Mrs. Pierce was at the first till, normally Janice's. He heard of her fainting fit.

'I wish she'd rung me. I'd have taken her home.'

The woman didn't answer.

'I'll go and see how she is.'

There was a degree of resentment in the woman's face that seemed inappropriate to the occasion; she'd be peeved at being short-handed, Alan decided. To conciliate her, he said:

'Look, I must apologize for nodding off last night at the séance. You will explain that I was over-tired, if you see Mrs. Worrall, won't you?'

The woman didn't answer, not at once. She seemed to have trouble in finding words.

'Yes, I will,' she said slowly after a full minute.

'Good! I'll send Jan back to work as soon as she's well.'

Alan left the shop feeling worse for the encounter. Some of his doubts returned.

# 7

Alan went home early. Janice was in bed, face down, her clothes strewn about the bedroom, skirt on the Persian rug, one shoe on the dressing table, the flowered bra crumpled beside the lamp.

She wore her yellow nightdress.

'Jan?' said Alan.

She was as still as a corpse. Alan touched her, half-expecting the white skin of her shoulder to be flaccid and cold.

'Jan? Jan!'

There was no response. Alan tugged at her still form, turning her in the billowing clouds of duvet. Her eyes were closed.

'*Jan!*'

She had pale lips normally, but not now. They were full, and bright red, like a peachy forties pin-up. There was something unhealthy about her.

Alan saw that she was breathing regularly. Her heart throbbed as he leant over her. He patted her hands and pushed a few stray blonde hairs from her face.

'Jan,' he tried again, 'I know you're not asleep.'

He meant that he was afraid that she had fallen into some kind of trance again, but he couldn't say so. Jan had to be asleep.

He considered asking the local G.P. to look at her. He visualized the encounter: 'Now what does she imagine is wrong with her this time, d'ye suppose?', for Janice was a constant visitor to the surgery. No, no doctor.

He said, 'I expect you'd like to be left, Jan. I'll go down now.'

So he watched television for a few hours, then when he slid into bed beside his wife and put an arm around her, he was profoundly grateful to hear a small sigh of pleasure at his touch.

His dreams were bad. He had an impression of chill and damp, darkness, and the seeping dankness of newly-turned earth. Janice was in the dream. She was in the pale yellow nightdress she didn't often wear, for it was long and billowy and not quite right for her pale complexion.

In the dream, it floated around her as she raised herself from the ground, and then the dream switched abruptly to the bedroom and then to where Janice was standing beside the bed; and she was naked again, but there was no hint of sexual display about her, for she was moving quickly and decisively, bundling something and easing a drawer back: and then Alan realized he was awake.

'Jan?'

'Yes, love?'

He meant to ask why she was changing her nightdress in the dim light of early morning, but he couldn't; no direct questions, certainly none about her nocturnal habits.

'Anything wrong?'

'No.'

She slid into bed and pulled the duvet around her. He didn't object, though his feet were uncovered.

After a while, he said: 'There's nothing wrong, is there? You had to come home from the shop. And you slept a long time.'

She didn't answer.

'You do feel all right, Jan? There's nothing worrying you, is there?'

'No, it's just that I had a migraine this afternoon. I took one of Myra's tablets and slept through.' She snuggled closer to him. 'It's nice to have someone worrying about you.'

Alan Charnock closed his mind tight. You worry too much, he told himself. Things were fine. All his life he had suffered from a mild anxiety state, and he knew what to do about it. Tell yourself, over and over again, that things were all right. And so he slept, peacefully, this time.

She was up before him. Alan heard a plate or a saucer shatter as she unloaded the dishwasher. Then the frying pan banged and a gushing sensation of pity and pleasure flooded him. Dear Jan. He climbed out of bed, quickly did his usual pressups, and found a clean shirt. Bacon and coffee smells permeated the stairs and landing.

The new shirt was blue, striped, and he paused, thinking about a tie to go with it. That one Janice's mother had given him last Christmas. Where was it? In Janice's drawer?

He felt amongst cool underclothes for the still-packaged tie. There. And something else, at the back of the drawer. Some sort of artificial fibre, lots of lace, and a hardness on the material. Puzzled, he pulled it into the light.

The nightdress was blotched rust-red.

An especial horror began to fill him. First, there was Janice in the yellow nightdress. He had turned her limp, sleeping body, when he had returned to the house the evening before. Next, the dream that had turned out not to be a dream, for it had ended where his waking state had taken over, at the point where Janice was in the bedroom; and she had been slipping out of a billowing cloud of material as she stood in the moonlight. But that was not all. Janice had hidden it from him.

He let a sleeve fall from his fingers. The yellow nightdress fluttered down. It was blotched by rust-red stains. They speckled the hem. Patches disfigured the bodice and skirt. The sleeves were daubed, as if dipped in gore.

'It can't be blood,' said Alan aloud. 'No!'

'Breakfast's ready!' called his wife.

After a while, he heard her footsteps on the thick carpet. 'Alan?'

Somehow he bundled the nightdress back into the drawer.

Janice smiled at him as she opened the door of their bedroom. 'You look as though you've seen a ghost, Alan.'

'I'm a bit off-colour. My stomach.'

'You'd better eat something. It's all ready, love.'

'I'll get my dressing gown,' he said, masking his anxieties.

Somehow he managed to get through the bacon and eggs and swilled the harsh coffee down on top of the bile that was rising to meet it.

Janice looked so *normal*.

Her conversation ran on the things they usually talked about. A new suit she'd seen at the boutique. The Bentleys had painted their bathroom green. The cracked paving in the garden that must be replaced. Nothing about a gore-stained nightdress.

He didn't ask. Instead, he delayed going to the office so he could drop Jan at the shop. She said her migraine had gone and that the graze on the side of her head didn't trouble her; Alan offered to take her to lunch, but she seemed to think she should cut her lunch-hour to make up for her absence the day before. Jan was thoughtful like that. He got the car out. She came to the door.

And then he had to say something to her. He called: 'How's your hand?'

Janice laughed. 'Look! It's better — see it was only a rash.'

The palm was clean and clear. Alan's heart thumped dangerously.

'Oh, good.' He turned away. 'I'm a bit shaky this morning.'

'You'll have to take things easy,' said Janice. 'You have got that ulcer, dear.'

Alan drove away fast.

# 8

On Monday, Alan Charnock made an appointment with Dr. McFaddyen.

The G.P. detested his patients, most of all the kind of neurotic he had in front of him. He looked up over steel-rimmed spectacles, a wizened, frog-featured man:

'Aye?' Rudeness made for shorter surgery hours.

'I'm Mr. Charnock,' said Alan. 'I keep getting bilious attacks. I've had a nervous stomach for along time.'

'Didn't I give you a diet-sheet some while ago, man?'

'I've kept to it, Doctor.'

'I suppose ye'll be wanting to go for X-ray. Not that I think it'll do ye any guid. These belly cramps don't come and go. Ye're stuck with them.'

'I didn't come about my ulcer attacks.' Alan waited. 'I keep getting these dreams.'

'What kind of dreams?'

'They frighten me to death.'

The sincerity of his manner impressed McFaddyen. But there were thirty more patients after this one.

'Aye?'

'And I don't think it's altogether dreams. It's my wife as well.'

'I couldn't give ye any pills for her!'

'I don't want any, Doctor. All I want is to ask if I'm going crazy.'

'And are ye?'

'No! I saw this — this *thing* — at the séance, in a sort of dream. Maybe a hallucination. It was composed of blobs of something, yes, it looked like hazy bits of material floating there. But they were alive! I can't properly describe it, but it seemed that something living had been shaken into pieces and was reforming again.'

Alan Charnock gestured to show what he meant.

'And there was a head. Definitely a head. Christ, what a thing! And it spoke, Doctor — the thing started to talk. Not talk exactly, though. Bits of words, fragments of sound. I think that's it, really. But talking! And Janice was moaning to it, just as if it was another person! And that's not all!'

'Aye?'

'It was two nights after we went to the séance, Doctor. I was awakened in the night. It was Janice. She wasn't in bed — I felt around for her, and I knew she'd gone. She was standing by the window, with the curtains open — and it wasn't the first time she'd stood in the moonlight. No! I didn't dare move. I know it wasn't a dream, because I heard a car arrive. The Baines-Ogdens' car. It has a loose exhaust that makes a distinctive sound. I know it isn't a dream. I checked next day, and they had come back late. They'd been to a party.'

The doctor nodded as if in agreement. Encouraged. Alan went on:

'You see, I know it's not hallucinations! I think I'm sick, but I'm sure Jan's a good deal sicker.' Alan's voice quivered. 'I know I'm not crazy, but it's getting so much worse! She hid the nightdress, and I know it's because of the blood.'

'I'll give ye some sleeping pills.'

'I don't need — '

'Another thing. Do ye take any exercise? Or do ye sit on your airse all day?'

'It is a sedentary kind of job.'

'Think about taking up golf — but don't start the wife at it! She'll never be away from the course.'

McFaddyen pushed across a prescription.

'Come back in a month. Guidnight to ye!'

Alan had felt humiliated at the doctor's fairly contemptuous dismissal of his problems, but he conceded McFaddyen's main point. Physical exertion might help. He hadn't taken much exercise in the past months, and he was becoming lax-muscled; so he worked in the garden for a couple of hours each evening, and began stripping the wallpaper in the spare bedroom, Janice approved. Their life resumed its even and uneventful tenor. The pills helped. Alan slept heavily without any grim dreams for three nights.

Alan had been dreading Thursday. A week ago the horror had begun.

'Maybe we could go out to see your mother? We haven't been for three weeks.'

'I don't think so, Alan. I'd like to have a quiet evening, Alan.'

He could hardly believe it. 'Stay in?'

'Why not? You weren't thinking of going out, were you?' And Janice smiled in that special way.

The nightmare was over. After all, it had only been a passing thing, probably a production of his own mind. McFaddyen was right. A little exercise and a few good nights' sleep. That was all it needed.

'You didn't want to go to the Spiritualist church again, did you, Alan?' Janice was looking at him cautiously. 'I didn't think much of it. But if you want to go?'

'No! No. Jan — not at all.'

He saw that they could talk it over. 'Then we'll stay in. That was a queer business, though,' he said, ready to reveal most of what had passed through his mind. 'I began to think you were a bit affected — '

Janice's smile faded. 'Why me, Alan?'

'Well, it did seem a bit odd, Jan! I

mean, when we got back, you in the lounge, love!'

'Well?'

'On the settee!'

'Was that wrong?'

Alan felt excited. 'No, Jan — but the curtains were open!'

'I didn't notice.'

'And before that, you weren't wearing a stitch in the garden.'

'I'd left the washing out.'

'But the neighbours might have seen you! And what were you doing out there?' Janice's eyes seemed to grow larger. Alan's new-found confidence evaporated.

'What did you think I was doing, love?'

Alan Charnock's mouth dried. 'Getting the washing in.'

'And you don't care about the neighbours, do you?'

'No.'

'Is there anything wrong, Alan?'

'No.'

'You're behaving a bit odd lately, love. Take two sleeping pills tonight.'

'Yes, Jan.'

'There's that paving stone to get up

when you've had some tea.'

'I'll do it.'

'And try to relax, love.'

Jan was smiling at him again, so Alan repeated his private incantation: *stop worrying, stop worrying, stop worrying!*

Later he was aware of the Baines-Ogden woman watching him as he reset the paving stone. He had always disliked her. She was large, and over-confident for her years. He doubted if she was more than twenty-two or three, yet she had the presence of a woman twice her age. He sneaked a glance as he bent.

She was watching him.

Two or three minutes passed and still she hadn't gone away. It was impossible to keep his back to her for longer. When he faced her, she said, without preamble:

'I've found Tim.'

'Tim. Oh.' More was expected of him. 'Oh, good.'

'He's been missing.'

Alan could vaguely recall its morning yappings. And that they had stopped. Too many people had dogs on the estate. It was one of the problems of suburban life, this pet-thing of the British.

'I've told the police,' said the woman, with barely suppressed anger. 'I think whoever's done it should go to jail. If I had my way I'd shoot them. To do a thing like that to a boy's pet!'

'I didn't know,' said Alan.

He looked down at the lawn and recalled the way the moonlight had caught the neat newly-mown parallels. The silver lines and Janice: and the whimpering animal with its belly on the ground: but that had been a week ago!

'I'm glad you've got him back. So long as there's no harm done.'

The Baines-Ogden woman opened her mouth wide: 'No harm? No harm done!' She was becoming almost hysterical. He badly wanted to walk away.

'He's dead!'

Alan felt himself becoming faint. 'Run over?'

'Killed! Cut up and killed! That's why the police are coming, Mr. Charnock! And if I ever find out who's done it, I'll get a gun and shoot them!'

Alan had an impression of a child

howling at her skirts. She turned away, a large, white-faced woman, shaking with rage. Alan trembled helplessly. It was half-an-hour before he could face his wife.

'You're tired, Alan,' she said. 'I think we both could do with an early night.'

They watched television. Janice tried to enter into conversation with him, but Alan could only answer in monosyllables. Visions tumbled through his mind as he watched the clever dancers and the showy singers. Jokes sparkled on the screen, but the memory of the knife and the moonlight stopped any kind of response from Alan. Janice watched him. When he drank his nightcap, she put out a second lot of sleeping pills. Laughter welled up inside her, tearing into her lungs and only stopping at her lips. But it wasn't the time for roaring laughter, not yet.

Alan swallowed the pills and went to bed at ten o'clock. Again he slept heavily, but not for long. The heavy drugs set up a chemical imbalance and failed in their work, for about an hour after midnight he

shuddered into wakefulness with a fero-
cious headache and a raging thirst.

He felt cautiously for Jan's sleeping
form, only half aware of what he was
doing. There was warmth, but no woman.
Jan had gone. Alan Charnock felt himself
shaking. It had happened again. He
remembered the gore-stained nightdress.

'Jan?' he whispered.

He listened for the noise of movement.
There was only the faint sound of water
bubbling somewhere in an air-blocked
pipe. No floorboards creaked. He pushed
the duvet aside and stepped out of bed.

He badly needed water. Groggily, he
inched his way across the floor. The room
was dark. He found the bedroom door
half-open.

'Are you there?' he called quietly.

As he said it, he heard the front door
swish open.

Abruptly, terror seized him. It froze his
guts, checked the urgent beating of
his heart, and brought a choked cry to his
lips. Someone had come into the house.
He listened as his heart raced to make up
for that moment of cessation.

Light steps tapped across the hall and into the kitchen. Water splashed into the sink, and a plug was pulled. It was Jan, unquestionably Jan.

At an hour or two after midnight, Alan Charnock's wife was returning from a visit.

'Where?' breathed Alan. 'Where's she been?'

Janice stepped about the kitchen. Alan heard a rattle of pots.

Then she walked from the kitchen to the hall. The lights went out, and Alan heard her step on the stairs. In seconds he was back in bed, rigid, questioning, sweating, and afraid to open his eyes. Janice slid noiselessly into bed.

For hours he lay like that, Janice sleeping beside him — asleep, he was sure, for he could hear the sound of deep, contented breathing.

When daylight filtered through the curtains — maybe five-thirty or a little afterwards — he had some kind of excuse to get up. His movements were those of an automaton, a well-oiled, silent machine.

Out of bed, downstairs, kettle switched on (already half-full) milk from the fridge. He was in the act of closing the fridge door when the stench hit him.

It was literally nauseating, for bile spewed from his stomach into his mouth. He ran for the sink, vomited, and ran the water to clear the mess. The fridge door hung open.

'Jesus!' Alan breathed.

The stench came from the lower shelf. He looked for its source. Four packets of butter; one of margarine; one of lard; a half-Edam. He cleared a space and looked in, though the wicked stench again made him retch. There was a newspaper-wrapped packet.

And it stank abominably.

Something had gone rotten overnight.

It must be crawling with maggots. Yet the fridge was cold. Alan pushed aside the butter. A sharp command startled him.

'I'll see to that!'

'Ah — this stink! I was — '

Alan might have had the showdown at this point, had not Janice slammed the fridge door. He withdrew his fingers just in time to save them from being crushed. He opened his mouth and then he saw his wife's hands. The nails were grimed and broken, the skin raw and blistered.

Janice was fastidious about her personal appearance. Her long delicate fingers were always beautifully manicured.

'What have you been doing to your hands, Jan?'

In that moment, he felt he had never begun to know her.

'My hands?'

Her voice was low and caressing. Her eyes blazed with a frightening intensity. She looked down at the jagged nails. Alan Charnock swallowed saliva. The stench was still in his nostrils, and he had seen its source: the newspaper-wrapped package. Jan was furious because he was downstairs so early; and searching in the fridge; and asking about her hands.

'What's the matter with my hands, Alan?' she asked, still in that low voice. Again she looked at him, holding his gaze and as she did so the eyes seemed to widen and the pupils began to dissolve into a pit of golden emptiness in which all feeling vanished and where only nameless horror remained. Alan's mind reeled.

'Look at my hands,' said Jan softly.

Alan looked away from the fiery yet empty eyes.

He saw the long, sensitive fingers. And the nails. The jagged edges were gone, and there was no sign of a blemish.

He shook his head, dizzy and unsure.

'I thought I saw — '

For a moment there was a blurring of the fingers. One nail split even as he looked.

'What, Alan?'

Alan shuddered, and the blurring cleared. The fingers were perfect.

'Nothing, Jan.'

'Go back to bed.'

Her voice grated dully on his troubled, tormented mind. He stumbled away, desperately trying to blot out what was becoming more and more obvious: Janice wasn't ill. Nor was he. The trouble had begun with the séance.

'Dear God,' Alan whispered, 'what can I do?'

# 9

In the event, Alan went to the library. The lady assistant, approving of his tall figure and good looks, led him to the Contemporary Religions shelf.

'Thanks, I can manage now,' said Alan.

'Oh, very well. But you'll ask if there's anything I can do?'

Alan didn't hear. The assistant decided he had a weak chin.

Only one of the reference books mentioned séances, and that a heavy, mock-leather volume of some age. It was the nineteenth-century Samuel Hoigges' definitive work, 'The Curtain of Dark'. Alan's trembling fingers moved down the index: 'Séances'. Hoigges disapproved. He classified Spiritualists with impostors and worse.

'Those that practise divination and seek to find wonders should beware,' wrote Hoigges. 'The calling of spirits at Séances is irreligious and full of peril.

There are dangers in the Great Void between this World and the Life to Come. To summon those that have gone before is to invite the attentions of the dead husks that roam the outer darkness. There are demons beyond the dark curtains of death ready to answer the summons of the charlatan practitioners of the cult called Spiritualism. Frequently ignorant and uneducated persons, they are either unaware of the terrible dangers of their craft, or, knowing those dangers, perniciously imperil their gullible followers. The demons of the void are not to be trifled with. Only depravity, torment and death await the victims of the dark forces.'

Alan groaned quietly. *The dark forces.* He looked down at his hands. He had the impression, momentarily, of Janice's hands, roughened and with those mud-rimmed, broken nails. He read on:

'They roam the night, infected by the demonic being within looking for the ghastly appurtenances of the Black Arts. The desolate places are their home, and the graveyard their treasure-house. Strange powers are theirs, and unnatural potencies. They indulge in the vilest of practices too horrible to describe, so that the demon might be confirmed in its possession of the afflicted soul. The mercenary spirit-raisers have much to answer for. It is the very soul of the victim that is at risk.'

Alan let the book clatter to the floor.

'Please be careful with the stock,' he heard dimly.

'At least you might pick it up,' the assistant said sharply.

Oblivious of her genteel disgust he strode out. The rain drove into his face, making a liar of the previous days that had seemed to herald summer. *Depravity. Torment. Death.* The words blazed in his mind. Jan had to be helped, and at once.

The shop steamed, full of wet shoppers. Alan had to wait until a woman arranged her three children in a trolley. He pushed past and made for a cash-desk.

'Where's Janice?' he asked one of the young assistants.

'I don't know. Oh, it's Mr. Charnock.

Where's Jan?' she called across a stack of tinned food.

'Gone home,' said another young girl.

'She's gone home,' the girl said to Alan's back.

He drove home in a careful frenzy. The estate was grey and empty of life, but he noticed glimpses of women's faces at curtains.

'Jan!' he roared as he opened the front door.

'Jan!' he yelled in the bedroom.

There was a woman's tidiness about the rooms; not a thing was out of place.

'Janice?' he said in the kitchen.

He had to open the fridge. Half-memories and grim conjectures struggled in his mind. It took courage to look inside.

He felt his mind exploding. He looked at his hands and saw them as vast, spadelike tools digging into the recesses of the fridge.

The package was gone. A lingering stench remained. Alan began to reason. Jan could have pitched it into the refuse-bin. Cheese, perhaps? One of the riper French cheeses she sometimes brought back from the shop?

'Jan?' he called again.

'She might be worse,' he heard himself saying. 'She's not here — where's she gone?'

It needed no decision. He turned the Rover and drove fast to the shop. Linda Pierce was at the cash desk. She flinched as he bent over her, and he knew that his neurotic terror communicated itself to her.

'Have you seen Jan? Did she say she'd go home?' he asked, struggling to appear calm.

'She asked for the afternoon off.'

'Why? Was she ill?'

'I don't think so.'

'Don't you know?'

Customers began to complain. Alan saw the three children in the trolley. All were eating chocolate.

'Mr. Charnock, I've got to serve now.'

'Just a minute, Linda! Where's the manager? Does he know where she's gone?'

'He doesn't come in today.'

'So you gave her the afternoon off?'

The woman was badly troubled. 'Janice had a few days' holiday to come, Mr. Charnock. I said she could go.'

'Go where? Mrs. Pierce, I've got to find her!'

The customers had ceased to nudge one another along.

'I can't see how I can help. And we're very busy, Mr. Charnock.'

'Why did she want the afternoon off?' Alan said fiercely. 'You do know — she'd tell you!'

'No, she didn't — '

'Tell me!'

Tears trickled through the patchwork of make-up. Women in the queue saw and began to murmur. It was becoming disagreeable. Then Mrs. Pierce gave in.

'Mrs. Worrall's.'

Details began to fall into place against a general pattern of aberrant behaviour. Blood and darkness. The filthy language. Janice standing like an age-old statue in the moonlight.

'Where does she live?'

Alan spoke gently now, for he had control of himself.

'Sixteen Charlton Lane — and don't — '

Alan left the rest of her words hanging in the steamy air. Charlton Lane: he knew it. Half-derelict, due for demolition within the year. It had been a solid, middle-class area a hundred years before, with bow-fronted houses and porches with delicately-painted tiles. It would take ten minutes or so to reach it.

The screaming voices in Alan Charnock's head would not be stilled. He could see her strange eyes as they had been the morning after the episode of the yellow nightdress. He had been sure her hands were raw and blistered, the nails torn, but after looking into her eyes, they were whole. He had seen, and then not seen. She had that power.

Unbidden words rose to his lips. The bile rose in his stomach. Only with difficulty did he control the smooth, heavy car.

Through the streaming rain, he made out the numbers on the doors. Forty-six. Forty-four. He drove on, spitting the bile into a paper tissue. Eighteen, abandoned and boarded up to deter vandals. Sixteen.

He switched off the ignition and stared at the dark-curtained bow-windows. Janice here!

'I've got to go in,' Alan told himself.

The green door was unlocked. He pushed and it slid open noiselessly, to reveal a long hallway. There was a light from a high window. There was an alien stench. Stale cooking smells, the aroma of years of poor living, and, mixed with these, the heady and aromatic odours of the night of the séance.

Alan made himself walk along the dingy hall. Two doors were closed, brown-painted and identical. The layout was familiar. There was a front parlour and a general purpose living room which would abut onto a kitchen-scullery. Where was Janice?

Very conscious of his shaking hands, Alan listened. He heard rain on the skylight, and a van in the street outside. There was no sound or hint of occupancy. Linda Pierce was wrong.

And then he heard something.

When it came, his legs almost gave way. It would have been comical in another situation, the tall man with the haggard face suddenly weak at the knees.

There was a faint moaning sound. It came from the parlour. It was a deeply disturbing noise, like the faint sound of a night creature heard over huge distances. It trailed away.

*Janice?*

Janice, ill? Alan put out a hand to the doorknob. He couldn't force himself to touch it. Sweating coldly, he waited.

The strange moaning began again, louder. It increased in volume and became higher in pitch. As it did so, the stink of corruption filled the hallway.

It was the noisome stench from the fridge. The rotted cheese. Or whatever it was. Subtly, the appalling stench blended with other odours into a terrible miasma, the stench of the charnel house.

The moaning became a low and hopeless keening. And then a new sound began to break the eerie silence of the old house. Words half-heard in the séance snatched at Alan's consciousness. He was sick to the heart, dizzy, terrified and quite unable to move. The words became a sly, sensuous and horrible incantation.

Alan knew the voice and why it pleaded. He refused to believe it. Janice couldn't — *couldn't* call on things from the darkness! Not sweet Janice, not the woman he had married!

Gutturals answered. There were more than two in the unseen room. The low and hopeless moaning came from the medium, and Janice's voice was unmistakable (but *could* she say those weird and bizarre phrases — could she?); and there was the heavy, iron voice of the other.

'Who's in there?' Alan called.

His words were lost in an upsurge of noise. The deep voice became a booming, with the cries of the medium as counterpoint. And Janice (it was Janice, Alan realized despairingly) was shouting wildly again, terrible cries of distress and longing.

'Oh, Christ help me!' groaned Alan Charnock, 'Dear Christ, help me!'

He reeled and half-fell. Without realizing it, he steadied himself and in doing so, the door handle turned in his shaking grasp. The door swung inwards a few inches.

Alan Charnock knew then that his wife was possessed.

He saw the frightful scene for perhaps ten seconds, but every detail was engraved on his mind: the chalked pentacle, the heaps of slimy detritus at its points; the flickering lights of candles; the dull sheen of nude flesh; the horror in the medium's upturned eyes; the wild impatience of Janice's beseeching stance. It was the strange dream again, but worse, for the gruesome appurtenances of the Black Arts littered the room, and the shadow in the corner beyond the candlelight could not be human.

Mrs. Worrall was in a state of shock. Her face was grey-white as she sat in a sagging armchair, head resting on its back, her hands raised as if to ward off the evil presence there. Janice knelt, her hands high above her head. In the poor light, Alan saw that she was streaked with red-brown pigment. Breasts, belly, and her face too, all daubed grotesquely with markings that were neither writing nor pictures.

Neither woman noticed Alan.

The medium's mouth came open, but no sound came. Janice yelled something, maybe an evil prayer. She was watching the dark shadow.

Grey-black, the thing had more definition than before. There was a head, clearly a head. Flaring nostrils seemed to open wide as Janice yelled. A mouth gaped and the booming and insane grunts came out with appalling force. Alan felt himself sliding forward. His terror checked the fall. Even as he began to close his eyes, he saw eyes, red as coals, glaring at Janice's swaying, streaked form. Tight ears bunched close to the appalling head. There was a hint of greasy bowed shoulders and a beast's hide.

And then it began to fade. Janice leapt to her feet, and screamed at the medium:

'Tell me how, you bitch, how! How can I get my love to stay, you sickening cow! How! Tell me, or I'll poison you, you useless great fat sow! Tell me — look at him, he's going again, he's lost, lost, lost!

Lost and Kelipoth! *Kelipoth!*'

Her voice trailed away on a despairing note.

It was nightmarish, so it had to be a nightmare. Trauma, Alan decided, as the mind's defensive processes began to operate. It had to be unbelievable. Had to be. It couldn't be Janice, so stop worrying. Couldn't be Mrs. Worrall summoning a demon. She was a charlatan, nothing more.

But the shadowy beast?

It was an aerosol. Jerry was right. She kept the stuff concealed and sprayed the grotesque shape. That was why it didn't last long.

Mrs. Worrall stirred.

'Oh, don't!' she breathed. 'You're killing me — I haven't got the strength to hold the shell — haven't got the strength. It will kill me if I try — '

'Try again, sow!'

Janice's face was quite inhuman. Bestial. Her actions were those of an animal, quick as thought. She bent her smooth, long legs, and flung something into the moaning, tear-streaked face of the medium.

93

A filthy stench filled the room. Alan shrank back. The medium opened her mouth and vomited in a yellow stream.

'Try, cow! Try, you stupid fat sow! Get my lover from the dark, or I'll cut your guts out!'

Mrs. Worrall put her hands up to ward off the threat.

Alan Charnock began to make the kind of moaning sound he had heard from the medium, but he was unaware of it. His wife growled like a beast, and then pleaded like a young girl as the shape grew stronger:

'Stay, only stay, my love, my great king, my own one, my heart, my love, my life! Get him to stay, you useless sow!'

Alan found himself speaking:

'You shouldn't say things like that, Janice. You're sick. Get some clothes on. We'll go home. I'll put you to bed.'

Mrs. Worrall screamed, and the half-formed shoulders heaved as the bull-like voice bellowed back to her. Its uncouth words were like splinters of iron in the room, grim and brutal noises, full of hope and confidence, yet with an underlying panic. Janice yelled in ecstasy and her whole body writhed with a fluid, languid, powerful grace that filled her husband with a kind of sick sexuality.

'Jan?' he whispered.

She couldn't hear. Every fibre of her being strained to interpret the jangling orders of the thing in the darkness. Joy radiated from her. The bizarre patterns on her body seemed possessed of a life of their own, for, as she moved, they wove a complex and hypnotic pattern that meant fulfilment and life, joy and a furious lust. There was a climax of a kind, too.

'Yes, yes!' she screamed. 'I see it now — blood and the power! Blood and the life for the emptiness! I see it, my King! Yes, yes! No longer dead and lost and Kelipoth!'

A weird and horrible grating like the laughter of a withered and long-dead corpse filled the room. Janice put her hands to her face and began giggling. Helplessly, she allowed the giggling fit to shake her body. She might have been a naughty schoolgirl. Whimpers of laughter forced their way into Alan's throat in sympathy with his wife's grotesque giggles.

She was shaking with relief, Alan realized. And the shadow in the corner had gone.

Alan watched, quite unable to move or to speak. He saw Janice look down at her body, and watched as she stroked the cabbalistic signs. They merged into ugly rusted blotches as she rubbed at them. Then she moved a pace towards the medium. Her naked foot slid on the heap of stinking mess at the pentagon's point.

'Mrs. Worrall?' she said.

Her voice was steady and normal.

The medium's face remained frozen in a rictus of horror. Her eyes rolled once, twice.

'You weren't bad at all, Mrs. Worrall,' said Janice soothingly. 'I was pleased with you today. Oh, yes, you had good vibrations, Mrs. Worrall, and I'm very grateful. We made good contact, though it didn't last long. Are you listening, Mrs. Worrall?'

The woman moved slightly. Her bulk shifted and her head slowly drooped until she faced the slim figure before her.

'Please?' she said in a slow, hesitant tone. 'Please, no more? Please? You've got real death in your soul.'

Janice didn't trouble to threaten her.

'I'll go. And you won't tell anyone about our little session, will you, Mrs. Worrall? We don't want anyone to start gossiping, do we?'

'No,' the woman sighed. 'Just the way you say, Missus. Lord God strike me dead if I speak a word. But please go. Please?'

If she turns now she'll see me, Alan said to himself. If she sees me, she'll know I've followed her. I've no choice.

With steady hands, he pulled the door to a narrow slit. Janice was in deadly danger. She must have help. That was the way Alan wanted to believe he thought. It would have been comforting to believe that he failed to interrupt the terrible scene because of some intention of learning more about the nature of Janice's possession. But that wasn't the reason.

Without properly admitting it, Alan sensed that his fears were for himself. He was frightened near to death, terrified to the point where he feared for his life. The words of Samuel Hoigges came back: 'There are demons beyond the dark curtains of death . . . '

Janice had called with the voice of power and authority. Her terrible domination of the grim performance marked her as possessed of strange authority and macabre power; 'Blood and the power,' she had screamed. 'Blood and the life.'

Alan Charnock stumbled away to his car. He feared that his wife would see him.

# 10

'We haven't seen you at the services for a few weeks,' the Reverend Unthank intoned. 'I was beginning to think you'd left the district. And how is Janice?'

Alan followed the Vicar of St. Ethelbert's into the smart lounge. The smell of fresh paint hung in the air, clean and wholesome. The Reverend Unthank was as tall as Alan, but broader and much fatter, with small green eyes peering above badly fitting gold-rimmed spectacles.

'You did say it was urgent when you rang, Mr. Charnock. Now, how can I be of service to you?'

It was going to sound so crazy. And he couldn't say it, after all.

'I think my — my house is haunted.'

'Really?' The priest looked genuinely interested. Alan nodded.

'Yes.'

'But you live on the Hurst Estate, don't

you? Those houses were built only about three or four years ago.'

'Six. We bought straightaway when we were married.'

'To Janice, now what was her name — don't tell me! Jones — that was it. How is she?'

'She's not been too well.' Alan sweated. 'She's seen it.'

'Really! You do surprise me! Only six years built, and a ghost in residence! Quite a mark of distinction, isn't it!'

'I thought — '

'Not that we've had much experience of the occult. There isn't much in the way of the supernatural in this part of the world. Who was that witch that used to live in a cave? Seventeenth century. Old Mother Demdike, that was it. Nasty bit of work from all accounts. They burned her. Anyone else haunted on the estate, by the way?'

The priest was discussing a haunting as if it were dry rot or rising damp. Flushing deeply, Alan put down his coffee untasted.

'It isn't the house, it's Janice!' he called

out loudly. 'It's Janice I came to see you about.'

'Ah?'

'We went to a séance. I saw the — *thing* there.'

'Not another ghost!'

'I'm serious,' said Alan. 'It frightened me out of my mind.'

'Really! You saw a ghost, then?' prompted Unthank.

'Not a ghost exactly. It was so indefinite — it was like a shape you can see in a dark corner, but it was forming whilst I watched.'

'That sounds ghost-like. Let's call it a manifestation, shall we? Did Janice see it?'

'She said she thought I was dreaming. But I think she really did see it as well.'

'We're getting into rather deep water, Mr. Charnock. Let's get this straight. It wasn't at your house after all?'

'I couldn't tell you about it at first. The first time it happened was at the Spiritualist church in Water Street.'

'I know it. And Janice was with you, but said she didn't see this — manifestation?'

'I've told you. She said I'd been dreaming.'

'And had you?'

Alan shook his head. 'I thought so. But not now, not after I saw it at the medium's house.' He shuddered at the memory.

'And now you've come to me.'

'I thought the Church might help.'

'Ah, Mr. Charnock, if only we in the Church had the certainty of our predecessors! If only we could apply simple remedies and dispose of the worries and stresses of our lives as in former days! But a few words of absolution or a stern exhortation to troublesome infestations of the mind and body are archaic usages now, I'm afraid.' He paused. 'You've had a bad fright, Mr. Charnock, but you'll get over it.'

'Mr. Unthank, I *saw* it! And at the house, Janice was screaming at it! And Mrs. Worrall was out of her mind with terror!'

'You have had a bad experience, Alan.' Mr. Unthank crossed his hands over his corpulent stomach. 'The Church doesn't take issue any more over religious controversies. The modern approach is the ecumenical one — we think that there are more ways of worshipping than through the prescribed ordinances of the Church of England. I believe that this Mrs. Worrall may be a good and devout woman, probably is, Alan. And when you tell me that your wife is interested in Spiritualism, I can only say that though I regret she doesn't direct her religious impulses towards her own church. You do see, my dear Alan, that this is a perfectly respectable and not improper activity, don't you?'

He rose to his feet.

'You don't believe I saw — '

'I didn't say I misdoubted your version of the experience, Alan!'

'But she can make things different — she made me think her nails were not torn after she'd been out in the night!'

'Alan, calm down!'

'There was blood on the nightdress and the dog had gone, and I'd seen her the first night with a knife — '

'Please. Alan!'

'I followed her when she went to Mrs. Worrall's. She'd got that poor old woman in a trance and she was calling up some devil from Hell! I'm going out of my mind with it all and no one believes a word . . . I don't know if I'm in a nightmare or awake!'

Alan Charnock got to his feet. His mind clouded with visions and the memory of abrupt guttural phrases and writhing cabbalistic signs.

'I don't know what I'm going to do,' he whispered.

'We'll have to work something out,' said Unthank.

'You mean you'll see her?'

'Of course! I christened Janice — of course I'll see her after what you've told me! Didn't you realize I would?'

'Soon?'

'Naturally! We can't have a nice couple like you troubled in this way.'

'I read about diabolical possession, Mr. Unthank. It said that there are wandering spirits which — '

'Wandering poppycock!' exclaimed Unthank. 'But very real at the moment to you, I'm sure! Now leave it with me! I'll see this Mrs. Worrall — what's the address?'

'Sixteen Charlton Lane.'

'Very well. I'll make time to visit her, and naturally I'll see Janice. Meanwhile, forget about it!'

Alan Charnock closed his eyes in relief. Anyone who saw Janice and Mrs. Worrall would have to recognize things for what they were.

'Thank you, Mr. Unthank.'

'Have you told anyone else about this, by the way?'

'One of the partners at the office. He just laughed and said it was an aerosol spray.'

'Ah. Anyone else?'

'Doctor McFaddyen. He gave me some sleeping pills and told me to take up golf.'

Mr. Unthank smiled. 'He has a pragmatic approach to psychosomatic ailments, has the doctor.'

'He's not fit to practise medicine!'

'That's too harsh, you know, Mr. Charnock. He's a busy man with a large list of hypochondriacs and malingerers.

Now take his advice — get some exercise, eat and sleep well. Leave the rest to me. Now go home and forget about it all. Yes?'

'Yes. And thank you.'

★   ★   ★

For two weeks Alan Charnock waited. Several times he rang the shop to ascertain if his wife was there. She was. At home, her behaviour was so normal that he felt his suspicions again crumbling. *Had* it been a hallucination?

The tablets McFaddyen had provided did something to relax his state of nervous tension, and Janice was particularly charming to him. There was no hint of the painted woman who had wailed at the grim shape.

At ten each evening he took his tablets and slept at once and though his dreams were troubled, he had no recollection of them when he awoke.

The Reverend Unthank hadn't called, that was the only troubling thing. Alan tensed every time the phone rang or the doorbell jangled. He knew, though, that

Unthank would help.

Then one evening Janice left a message with Myra Bentley. She would be home late. Alan was to cook himself eggs and bacon.

'Did she say why?'

Myra Bentley smiled. She pushed past Alan and turned on the grill.

'No. I'll cook your meal. Jim's had his. Go and sit down and read your paper.'

'But she didn't say anything about going anywhere? Didn't she say what time she'd be back?'

'No.'

Alan felt himself choking. 'She's gone to that poor Worrall woman's!'

Myra turned the bacon. 'Now why should Janice do that?'

In his relief, Alan told her. 'I've been out of my mind with worry, Myra. After the séance, Jan didn't act herself — if only you'd seen what I've seen! She's obsessed with this spirit business. She's been back to see the medium!'

'Did she tell you?'

'No! I got it from the woman at the shop — Mrs. Pierce. And she didn't want to tell me. She knows more — I swear she does. And I'll get it out of her! They've got poor Janice in a shocking state!'

Myra Bentley smiled. 'Jan knows what she's doing. Two eggs, Alan?'

Alan Charnock watched her deft movements. As she served the meal, he had the curious impression that her smile was not for him. She had always seemed a good-natured woman, but Myra Bentley looked particularly unpleasant at that moment. Doubts sprang afresh in his mind. He looked at the grilled bacon and thought of the stench from the package in the fridge.

When Myra Bentley left, he had to throw the meal away. *Where was Janice?* He rang the Reverend Unthank. Mrs. Unthank answered.

'It's Alan Charnock, Mrs. Unthank. I wonder if the Vicar's in?'

'I'm afraid not, no!'

'Do you know if he got in touch with Janice — my wife?'

'I really don't know, Mr. Charnock.'

'Has he been to see the medium yet? Mrs. Worrall — it's about a séance.'

'He did say something about trying to contact a Mrs. Worrall, but I don't think he was successful. Is there any message I can pass on?'

'No, no thanks.'

'I'm sure Mr. Unthank will call you. Goodnight.'

'Goodnight.' Alan put the phone down.

'She's gone to Mrs. Worrall's,' he said. 'She has!'

He ran out of the house, and drove to Charlton Lane. When he could control himself, he knocked at the door. There was no reply. The house echoed and re-echoed as he pounded the door.

A passing policeman stopped. Alan saw him and turned away, aware of the policeman's eyes as he drove off.

The house was empty. So where was Janice?

At home he could stand the strain no more. He had to stop worrying! Four of the tablets should be enough to blot out the doubts and the horror.

They were a temporary anodyne, for sometime in the grey dawn Alan Charnock heard the grating, diabolical voice of the unformed thing and his wife's low, soothing replies. He was heavily drugged, so the terror touched him only at the fringes of consciousness. Against his will, he dragged himself to the top of the stairs.

'*Kel — i — poth*!' the voice rang out. '*Kelipoth!*'

'Soon,' whispered Janice Charnock. 'Soon you live in blood and flesh, my king!'

Later a new voice joined in, but that might have been part of a dream:

'He said Mrs. Pierce sent him to Charlton Lane.'

'Did she?'

And Janice's voice was honey and gall, venom and cream.

'He's going to see her tomorrow,' the other female voice said, excitedly.

'Oh no,' said Janice, all honey. 'Oh no.'

The fear of death filled Alan. He returned to bed and willed himself back into the drugged oblivion he had awoken from.

# 11

The next day brought the worst of all.

Alan heard his wife splashing in the bathroom and then she called to ask if he felt well. When he didn't answer she called that she would bring him a tray.

Janice smiled down at him.

'Alan, pet, you've not slept well. You've terrible rings under your eyes. I'll catch the bus. It's Saturday, so you don't have to get up. Stay in bed, won't you?'

'Yes, Janice.'

Her eyes were smoky and, behind the smoke, blazing with power.

'Good,' she said.

He waited until she left the house, then dressed quickly. The coffee cooled, and the eggs congealed. He could not have swallowed any of it. He thought of Jan's thin hands on the foul-stinking package in the fridge.

He was quite sure she would not go to work. By now, he was too confused to believe that he was following her to save her from some nameless peril. The cumulative effect of sleeplessness, heavy drugs, and the bizarre experiences of the past weeks had numbed him. He followed Janice as a television watcher stares at a bad old movie, simply to get to the end. The bus stopped every few hundred yards. But he kept to it, leaving his mind blank of intention. He didn't consider her destination. Mrs. Worrall's, the Vicarage, some rendezvous with another occultist — it made no difference.

And, after all, she stayed on the bus until it reached the shopping centre of Mersey Pagnall.

Janice tripped off lightly. Her lithe legs flashed in the driving rain.

Alan got out of the car and waited.

She went into the supermarket and still he waited, not convinced that things would take their normal course. He traced her movements mentally, knowing the morning routine. Coat and handbag away, overall on, a visit to the ladies' room and then neatly tap-tapping her way through stacked shelves.

Five to nine. Janice, his wife, would be getting ready for the Saturday stint.

She returned to view after three minutes, but she didn't take her place at the till. She was smiling out into the rain, as if at Alan. Then Alan saw Linda Pierce die.

Events kaleidoscoped. They didn't become separate until afterwards. It was all so paralysingly fast. The blue and red bus braked. Linda Pierce jerked forward like a puppet, a doll with broken limbs, still screaming in a bubble of red froth.

There were separable elements, separable later, that is. Janice not at the till, but standing in the doorway of the supermarket and her eyes shimmering, golden and hazy, and staring beyond Alan. Alan turned. It was Linda Pierce. She began to say something but stopped. Her words trailed off to nothing, and she walked past Alan with quickening steps into the road — it must have taken perhaps two or three seconds in all. The greeting, then the moment when Janice's basilisk glare entranced her, and the uncoordinated steps into the path of the

113

tons of red and blue metal accelerating down the high street.

The bus stopped fifty yards away. It was obvious that the woman was dead, for her injuries were terrible. Alan choked back a sobbing noise, and a sick, crazy impulse to call out that Charlie would be glad. But he held back. He wanted to help in some way, yet he could not. He backed away, lost in the crowd.

It was Janice's eyes he could not face. He shook his head until his ears rang. There had been that odd smokiness, just as on the night when he had seen her nails broken and her hands raw. Things became what they were not when she stared in that way. He went home, driving slowly and unable to form any kind of plan.

He tried the doctor's pills and slept for a while, and, when he awoke, neat gin. Then he was excruciatingly sick and his head hurt abominably. Barely in possession of his faculties, he rang his wife shortly before the store was due to close for the evening.

'Janice?'

'What is it, Alan?'

'I wondered what time you'd be home.'

'Are you all right?' she asked calmly.

'Yes. Are you?'

How could she sound calm when the woman had been shattered that morning in the sweeping rain.

'Well, not altogether, Alan. We've had a terrible accident here — have you heard about Linda Pierce?'

Did she know that he had seen it?

'Mrs. Pierce?'

'She was killed this morning, Alan. Isn't it dreadful?'

'It's terrible, Jan.' He meant to ask why was she killed, but he couldn't say it. 'What happened?'

She couldn't have known he followed her.

'It was a road accident. She seemed to run under a bus.'

'She didn't seem a careless sort of person.'

'Alan, I can't stay talking. We're busy clearing up.'

'I suppose they'll give you the supervisor's job.'

'Temporarily only, Alan. Why?'

'Nothing.' Moved by an unknown impulse, he said: 'Be careful, Jan.'

There was a moment's silence. 'Oh yes, Alan. Take care too.'

'I rang the Reverend Unthank about you, love. I was worried about the séance the other night.'

'So that's why he wants to see me! I thought he sounded mysterious, but I guessed it was about doing some job at a fête. You know, when you have to run a stall or something.'

Jan's laughter rang down the telephone. It sent shivers through Alan.

'I'm seeing him tonight, Alan! I forgot to tell you. Of course, we're all very upset about poor Linda, but I think I'd better keep the appointment, don't you?'

'Yes,' said Alan.

'I'll be back as soon as I can. See you later!'

★   ★   ★

At eight Janice still hadn't returned.

On impulse, he rang the vicarage.

'I wonder if Janice is still talking to the Vicar?' he asked Mrs. Unthank.

'I couldn't say, Mr. Charnock. I've just returned after a day out. You seem rather upset again. Is there anything I can do?'

'I thought she was there.'

'I'm sorry to sound unhelpful again, but I really don't know, Mr. Charnock.'

She sounded tired, and Alan heard the sound of children squabbling. He thanked her and rang off.

He watched a film on television until the hammering music made his head ring.

At ten, he flung on an old raincoat and drove to the church.

Time had not been kind to St. Ethelbert's. The fifteenth-century tower needed re-facing. The main porch had once boasted a frieze of pilgrims and saints, but now only flaking limestone remained. Tombstones lurched at odd angles, and one of the buttresses was shored up by worm-eaten timber. The last fund-raising appeal had failed.

Alan pushed on the iron-barred oaken door. It swung away reluctantly but without a sound. There were no lights in the church, though towering Jacobean pulpit, pews, high altar, organ pipes and columns were clear enough as the street lighting filtered through the stained glass of the side-chapels. He waited, wet and deeply distressed. There was a low sound.

'Mr. Unthank?' said Alan.

Janice's voice rang out as if in answer:

'Come on, priest! *Come on!*'

Feminine laughter, high and wild, echoed around the roof. Alan was as still and cold as the stone all about him. *Janice?*

A male voice called something in a guttural voice. Janice yelled again:

'Kiss me, kiss me, priest, hold me — *kiss!*'

In a daze, Alan began to walk towards the source of the sound. It led him over the worn pile of the carpet between the rows of pews to the base of the elaborately carven pulpit. Jacobean and beautiful and big as a boat. Scuffling came from inside it.

'God help me!' someone called, and Alan recognized the voice of Mr.

Unthank. 'Christ, dear Lord, what has she done to me?'

The man groaned. Alan recognized his defeat.

'Again, priest!' screamed another triumphant and hateful female voice.

Alan recoiled from the new sound. It wasn't Janice.

'No!' bawled Unthank. 'Please, no!'

Aghast, Alan listened whilst the two women shrieked and Unthank moaned. He had to see, yet he dared not let the women know of his presence. Silently and with despair clutching his insides, he ran to the organ where he could see from deep shadow and himself remain unseen.

In the dim light, he watched the naked figures writhing in the wide pulpit. Alan recognized the second woman.

'Myra!' he called involuntarily.

Immediately, movement and noise stopped.

Unthank groaned and pushed the shorter, heavier woman aside. Janice slowly raised herself to her full height and looked directly at Alan.

'Alan?'

He was out of sight, in deep, heavy shadows. He felt his teeth juddering and his knees become gelatine. If he moved, he was finished. He knew it, with all the strength of his wildly thumping heart. Janice would not forgive him. The women were monsters, both of them.

Their souls were in the grip of what Hoigges had described, the thing from beyond the curtain of dark. Together, they had encompassed the ruin of the priest of St Ethelbert's.

If they found him, they would do worse to him. He knew it.

'I know you're there, Alan,' said Janice. 'Come here, darling. I want you — come here, Alan.' She giggled disgustingly. 'Myra wants to try you. Alan — come on!'

Again Alan was gripped by the same horror and shame he had felt on the night of the séance.

'It is you, Alan, isn't it?' called Myra Bentley. 'I do want you, darling — come to me!'

Alan sensed Unthank struggling with his clothes. The big man was sobbing.

'Going so soon?' Janice giggled.

'Any time, reverend!' said Myra sweetly.

'Alan?' called Janice as Unthank crawled down the steps of the pulpit.

'God help me!' sobbed Unthank, running from his church.

The women ignored him. They watched and waited.

'Maybe it wasn't him,' said Myra.

'I heard something,' said Janice. 'Honey, come to your loving wife — '

'We won't harm you,' cooed Myra. 'It will be marvellous, Alan!'

'I wonder,' said Janice, and Alan heard the iron inflection that was so unlike Janice, but which was now part of her.

'Maybe he's gone — if it was him,' said Myra, and Alan allowed his aching lungs a small amount of air.

'I wouldn't hurt you,' said Janice. 'Not if you were a good boy.'

'And kept your mouth shut!' snarled Myra Bentley.

'Otherwise,' Janice called softly. 'Otherwise, Alan, there are ways.'

He believed her. Three minutes passed in silence, with the two women waiting like hunting beasts in the dark.

'Out,' said Janice abruptly. 'It doesn't matter whether he's here or not. He's harmless. Besides, we must make the offering now. Kelipoth hungers — he must have life!'

Without another look in the direction of the altar, Janice and Myra dressed quickly and left the church. Alan saw the gilt Cross glimmering and allowed a small prayer to escape him. He prayed that they would not notice his car.

If they saw it, they would know, and they might return. He knew now that his wife had murdered Linda Pierce for what she might tell him. She and Myra Bentley had perverted the priest to prevent any interference with their activities.

What they intended was not to be thought of: it was enough — too much — that Janice had become possessed by a thing from the Pit. The Church had failed against it. There was no more to be done.

Regardless of his chronic ailment, he had to get drunk. What else?

A good citizen, Alan Charnock made sure that he would not be a danger to the public. He left the ignition keys in the glove compartment of the Rover and locked the doors.

He could not contemplate a return to his home. Drunk or sober, he knew he would not have the nerve to confront Janice. She was altogether too potent a force.

The nearest pub was only a few minutes' walk.

★　★　★

Alan saw himself in the bar mirror and shuddered at his reflection. It was an old bar, the mahogany and brass not replaced by plastic and chrome, the clientele working men mostly. Alan saw that he blended in fairly well, for his coat was soaked and he did not wear a tie. There was a fatigued and yellow look on his unshaven face. Methodically he set about getting drunk.

The roaring in his head soon stopped as he drank whisky, and when he felt the bile rising against it he forced it back with draughts of bitter beer. Someone began to argue over a game of dominoes. A buxom barmaid leant over to shout the quarreller into silence. She looked at Alan and a half-smile came to her lips. It was meant only as a gesture of greeting but Alan saw in her painted eyes and red lips the false and deadly glamour of Janice and Myra.

He edged away towards an unoccupied table.

An hour passed, and still he was not drunk. He had taken three large whiskies and three pints of beer. Normally that would have been enough to incapacitate him. The pub began to fill with middle-aged couples. One couple appeared before him, a short, burly man and his painfully thin wife. They had to ask twice before Alan understood that they wished to share the table.

Without meaning to, he began to tell them about the church. At first, they treated him with some respect, but his incoherent account made them uncomfortable.

'What's that about the Vicar?' asked the man.

'Our Vicar — St. Ethelbert's?' his wife asked.

And Alan groped for the words to say that the Reverend Unthank had defiled his own church with two young women.

'Have you been reading this in the paper?' demanded the man.

'Is it a joke — a story?' his wife suggested.

'It was Jan!' Alan got out. 'My Janice — I couldn't stop them — she killed that poor woman this morning — and if she'd seen me — she was naked — '

'Maybe you've had enough,' suggested the burly man.

He was offended. Alan recognized that he had gone beyond the bounds of decent confidentiality. The couple didn't know how to cope with a drunk whose face streamed with tears.

'Have you been ill?' someone else said.

Alan looked up. Time had passed again, and he knew that he had fallen unconscious whilst sitting there. The couple had removed themselves.

It was the landlord now. He knew what to do.

'Up you get. Can you walk? I'll give you a hand into the fresh air. You'll feel better. Up!'

Out in the street, Alan found that he could walk. It was an area with an abundance of pubs, and he managed to make himself presentable during the minutes it took to reach the next one. No one offered to speak to him. This was a sordid place where the market traders drank. There were groups of sharply-dressed teenagers, and solitary older men, very shabby, market odd-jobbers.

No one spoke to him. And yet the urge for human companionship drove him towards the bar again and again, if only to hear the uninterested barman ask for his order. He drank gin now, for the whisky fumes made him retch.

After three glasses, he tried to strike up a conversation with a red-faced, shabby man slumped across a table near his. He said that the rain was worse, and when the man didn't answer, he called that he'd seen the accident in the High Street.

The man turned and Alan Charnock remembered something.

'You were in the pub,' he said, clarity returning.

Ruane heaved himself up from the table.

'You were in the 'Coach and Horses',' said Alan. 'When Jan was there. I remember you. You spilled sherry over her.'

That was all he could remember. He drank the gin at a gulp and the moment of lucidity had passed. Fog crawled in front of his eyes, and his head whirled.

He looked up and saw the burly figure moving away from him. Suddenly he knew he could talk to the red-faced man. There had been a reaction in the bloodshot eyes. Alan lurched to his feet.

He bumped into a teenager who pushed him aside. Alan spun and cannoned off the bar. His arm felt as though it was broken, but he kept on, to the laughter of the young men.

'Wait!' he called into the darkness and the rain. 'Wait — you saw her! You saw the mark on her hand! It was there!'

The wind had got up. A bus swished by, confusing Alan with its lights and faces staring into the rain.

Alan shuddered and nursed his arm, for the burly man had gone and so had his need to speak to him. He was alone and deserted, lost as the paper swirling across market stalls and empty bus shelters.

He had the feeling that he and the despair within him were the only things left in the world, and that the black rain drove through and through him. He was lost, unspeakably lost and afraid.

An echo of Janice's terrible cry rang in his ears, the grim and unknown sounds she had wailed when the medium had seemed to be failing.

Hiding in a doorway only twenty yards away, Ruane felt his heart freeze. He had half-known it would be this night, and he had recognized the tall man with the gaunt face and despairing loneliness. He looked out.

'Help me!' came the eerie cry, and then Alan had seen him.

'Wait!'

Ruane stumbled away. It was a grotesque chase, one man half-drunk and ponderous, the other wholly drunk and yet given a maniacal strength. In a few strides, Ruane was in the young man's claw-like grip.

'You — you know!' sobbed Alan Charnock. 'You saw it — you knew the mark on her hand!'

'Get away, you fool!' bawled Ruane. 'I don't know what you're talking about. Away, away, man!'

Alan had him fast.

'I went to the priest when she'd killed the woman from the shop! But she made him rotten too — I saw her with the devil-mark on her, and so did you!'

Ruane exerted his brute strength and flung the young man away. Alan lay where he fell, his face strained and contorted. Ruane saw the horror in his eyes, and yet he could not offer help, for who was he to challenge the evil that stirred in the night?

Alan felt the fear of death in his soul, and repeated the grim cry that had come from his wife's lips:

'Kelipoth!' he wailed. '*Kelipoth!*'

'God in Heaven,' muttered Ruane. 'Where did you learn the Name of the Damned?'

# 12

A dreamy lassitude filled Janice as she left the church. The thing inside her began to murmur, as it could sometimes, thickly and without making sense, but with a great sweetness too. She moved slowly, listening to its unformed and unborn demands. She had never felt so powerful. She laughed with pleasure at the memory of what she had done.

'That priest!'

'It was easy!' Myra exploded.

Somewhere inside what was left of Janice's soul, a memory struggled.

'Alan — '

'What about Alan!' jeered Myra.

'Oh, my poor Alan — '

Then a raging torrent swamped her mind, and Janice began to giggle.

'I think he's trying to save me. Save me! *Me* — the One has chosen! Because He comes through me!'

Janice felt the thing swell. Was it like a

pregnancy? Belly full, heart leaping madly. She remembered what other women had told her. And then it became alarmed, and she had to grit her teeth against its agony that was hers too.

'Kelipoth!'

Janice felt her bones dissolve as it bayed its terror. It was the cry of the aborted.

'No!' she called back. 'Wait, my darling! There is life — there is blood for you, *blood*!'

★　★　★

Ruane had known the thing would find him. The knowledge had been with him since the night it had called out in malicious triumph across the shallow hills. And now, before him, was the first sign of its passing, this half-crazed man as lonely as death.

Ruane closed his eyes.

Why should it be him, Ruane, to take up the challenge?

'We'll get out of the rain,' he said.

They passed a group of white-faced women huddled outside a lighted shop.

Two police cars arrived and Ruane felt a nagging idea deep below the level of conscious thought, but it passed as soon as it came.

By the time they reached the transport café, Ruane was almost sober. The booze was in his bones, permeating every fibre, but he could think and reason, listen and plan. He guided Alan to a table.

'You did see it?' Alan said dully, as Ruane brought cups of tea.

'I saw it.'

'I did too, whatever the priest says!' He knew that Ruane could help him now. The knowledge that he was not alone brought a great peace. 'She can make things different, though. Can't she?'

Ruane recognized the uncertain logic of the drunk.

'Where is your wife now?' he asked, to keep the man from sliding into the inviting oblivion he himself knew so well.

'She was at the church.' Alan shuddered. 'With the other one. God knows where she is now!'

Ruane saw the torment and felt doubt. A sense of dread came too. Whatever terrorized the young man could communicate itself directly to others.

'So your wife is the one? And it began about a month ago?'

Alan nodded. 'Three weeks and three days. When we went to a séance.'

'Can you tell me about it?'

Alan's eyes began to shade over.

'Listen! The name you said — when you shouted tonight. Kelipoth — the name of the Devil's spawn! Where did you hear it? Where?' Ruane leant forward and shook Alan Charnock

Alan Charnock felt the blackness crowding in on him.

'You — can't — do — *anything*!'

Ruane sat with him as the hours of the night slipped away. Hour after hour passed, with the desperate young man slumped across the greasy-topped table. No one paid them any attention. Motorcyclists gathered in groups, haggard women came and went, night drivers had their cigarettes and tea and went on their way. Towards dawn, a police crew questioned the proprietor. Then they left too.

Ruane ordered two bacon sandwiches at five o'clock. He pushed one under Alan Charnock's nose.

'Wake up,' he said. 'You've slept enough.'

Alan jerked and awoke muttering to a crashing headache.

His spine creaked as he sat up. Dimly he recalled talking to Ruane.

'I'm sorry to give you this trouble,' he began to say. 'I didn't mean — '

'Do you know what 'Kelipoth' means? No. You've heard a possessed woman call on it, but why this name? I'll tell you.' Ruane was tired but not exhausted. During the night hours, he had considered what he should say. His conclusion was that the young man's state of mind could not be worse. Knowledge might help him.

He said:

' 'Kelipoth' is the shell of a spirit. It is empty, a husk, but it knows that it might live if it can gain possession of a human soul. Is this what has happened to your wife?'

Alan pushed the sandwich away.

134

'Eat it,' said Ruane. 'You look half-starved.'

To his own surprise, Alan Charnock could eat the food and enjoy it. He drank the tea. The pounding inside his head lessened.

'I saw her talking to it. The priest called it a manifestation. But he didn't know! He couldn't know what it was like, and he didn't believe it,' Alan smiled grimly. 'He does now.'

'I believe it,' said Ruane.

Alan could reason now. He saw a shabbily-dressed, red-faced man who might be sixty, or again, forty years of age. The face was square, with a heavy jaw and a nose that had been broken at some time. He could have been an itinerant labourer, for there was a trace of the brogue in his voice. However, he had been educated. Irish labourer or broken-down clerk? Alan gave up the puzzle. Whoever he was, there was no disputing the fact that he was a wreck.

And yet he had recognized the thing, had known it the moment it began to infect Janice's soul. He knew the terrible name too. Unbelievably, the man had responded to his drunken cries after the frightful experience in the church.

'Who are you?' asked Alan.

'Ruane.'

It wasn't enough.

'My name is Alan Charnock, and my wife is called Janice. You saw us on the night of the séance, and you recognized the mark on her. Now, what in God's name are you? A medium?'

'No. Just a man.'

'You know more about it than Unthank! You explain it better than the book I read — ' He broke off. 'That's it,' he said. 'You must be a priest.'

'Not now. I was in orders — once.'

Alan saw the pain in his eyes. He got up, confused and ashamed.

'No more bloody priests! I've had enough of them!'

'Go if you must,' said Ruane. 'But remember that the unclean thing is in your wife's soul, and there it will remain. And worse to come. She is possessed.'

Alan thought of Janice's slender figure and the way she smiled, innocent and warm and radiant. He remembered too the dazzling, sly and vicious smile when she told him at the séance that the fun was just beginning. Numbed, he sat down. It wasn't Janice that had shattered the medium, not Janice who perverted the Anglican priest in his own pulpit; but an iron-tongued, fearful presence that reeked of corruption.

'How could you tell?' said Alan.

'I could always smell out the deep and undying evil,' said Ruane. 'As a parish priest, I was a failure, but I knew the stench of evil.'

'You really think you can help me?'

'I don't know. Recognising evil isn't the same as defeating it.' Ruane looked down at his hands again. 'I don't know what you've been through, and I don't know what I can do for you. I was relieved of my duties for what the world calls 'scandalous behaviour', and since then I've been of no use to man or beast. I couldn't pass you by last night, though. Not when you called out like a lost soul.'

'It's Janice who's lost.'

'Tall and slim, with white hands,' said

Ruane. 'I remember her.'

'Yes. We were happy till the seance. Happy enough, anyway. It was a dull life, I suppose, but it satisfied me. We didn't want kids, not yet for a while, not until we'd seen something of life. We'd got all we needed — a house, a car, jobs we both liked. Why did we have to go to that seance?'

'Calm down. Can you tell me about it now? It's sometimes helpful to share a burden.'

'But what can you do afterwards? I thought a priest could help, but they they — ' He couldn't mouth the humiliating words. 'And you're not even a priest!'

Alan's anger and shame grew until it filled him. He got to his feet, bitterly furious with Ruane, and aware too that the man was not the cause of his distress.

'No,' said Ruane. 'Not even a priest.'

Alan Charnock left him, a bowed and fatigued middle-aged man with no pride and no desire for anything but the submergence of thought and pain.

The spurt of anger that had driven

Alan from the transport café didn't last. It had seemed enough to fuel a showdown with Janice, but by the time he had crossed the town square in the grey light of the morning, Alan Charnock knew he could not sustain the mood.

His wife had committed adultery and taunted him to his face. She had invited him to share sex with her friend, Myra.

And then she had contemptuously dismissed him when he dared not answer her. All of this — any of it — would have been enough to bring a normal man to a blood-rage.

Alan felt only a sick despair.

It wasn't Janice who honeyed those vile endearments from the oaken pulpit; no more than it was Janice whose eyes blazed at poor Linda Pierce across the wet street. Janice hadn't flung the horrible mess at the medium's contorted face, nor ripped the terrier open, nor transformed broken nails and raw hands to wholeness.

Not Janice.

It was the monster within.

He found himself wandering towards

his parked car. It seemed right to sit in it as the sun began to shine through the mist of dawn.

Without realizing it, Alan began to doze.

A light tapping filtered through his violent dreams; always the dreams were violent now, wild and lost dreams which left no trace of their passing but which were almost unendurable.

He blinked to consciousness. A fat uniformed patrolman was looking into the car. Alan wound down the window.

'Everything all right, sir?' said the policeman.

His mate joined him, a pink-faced youngster.

'Yes, I think so,' said Alan. They would be wondering whether it was worth their while breathalysing him. 'Why?'

'Spent the night in the car, sir?' asked the young one.

'No.'

'Not been home last night?'

'No. What's the trouble?'

They recognized the tone of authority, for Alan was used to dealing with officials.

'We're making inquiries about a missing child,' the fat patrolman said. 'We're
asking everybody hereabouts if they've
seen or heard anything — anything at all
— in the night.'

'Infant, sir,' said the young policeman.
'About eight months. Taken last night
quite near here. First baby-snatch we've
had in the area. Did you say you'd been
here all night, sir?'

'No. I was out. Most of the time I spent
in the transport café down there,' Alan
said, pointing.

'You wouldn't have seen anyone carry-
ing a child of about that age? Wrapped in
a blue shawl. A boy it was, sir,' said the fat
patrolman.

'Nasty business,' said the other.

'Yes.'

Visions grew in his mind. He thought
of a yellow nightdress blotched and hideous, and the thin blade in the moonlight.
There had been a terrible urgency in
Janice's instructions to Myra Bentley in
the church. But such things couldn't be.

'You got any kids, sir?' said the fat
patrolman.

'No.'

'If you remember anything, you'll contact the station, won't you, sir?' asked the young one.

*Tell them that Janice was possessed by a monster that demanded . . .*

'If I think of anything, I'll let you know.'

'We'd better have your name, sir,' said the fat patrolman. 'Just a formality.'

There was a cautious look on his face. Did they sense what he dared not think?

Alan gave his name and address. He knew they watched as he drove away.

*Ruane*, he said to himself. Why had he rejected the man? Why, when there was no one he could turn to! He thought of the crowd of women gathered about the lighted shop front the night before; that must have been where the infant was stolen. Janice had left the church minutes before. But he couldn't have told the police that, not when it was his own wife. It was only a bizarre coincidence that she should be in the neighbourhood at the time. Of course. He laughed at the idea and drove faster.

The ulcer reminded him of its presence with sharp jabs as the Rover hurtled around the tight bends of the estate.

*It wouldn't be Janice!* Not an infant.

Maybe a dog — he could begin to admit now that the Baines-Ogdens' dog might have been killed as part of a sacrificial ritual, because it was so much easier to accept than the other vileness. Maybe Jan was in the power of a terrible spirit, but that wouldn't cancel all her natural instincts. No.

'Jan!' he called when he unlocked the front door. 'Jan?'

He found her asleep in bed. She looked sixteen years old. Her fine blonde hair lay all about her head, giving her a virginal appearance. She stirred in her sleep.

'Jan!'

Her eyes opened reluctantly. They were large and moist, slightly protuberant, and entirely ordinary. Alan choked back his dread of her.

'Where've you been?' she demanded, wifely and querulous. 'You've been out all night!'

He was dumbfounded. She had seduced

the Reverend Unthank hours before, and she had not cared that he, her husband, watched from the shadows. And this yesterday, after guiding Linda Pierce to her death.

Alan gabbled fast:

'I've just been talking to the police — there's a baby missing. Stolen from a shop in the High Street last night. It was in a blue shawl. Jan, someone's taken a baby! Who could harm a child, Jan? Who'd want to steal a baby? Why should anyone do that? Jan?'

The other things could be forgotten. Alan began to realize that he had a capacity for self-deception. If nothing else happened, then he could, over a period of years, adjust to the rest.

But not the killing of a baby.

Jan smiled at him. 'I heard about it on the local radio station. Whilst you were out. Do you know I didn't get to sleep till three in the morning?'

There was a strangeness in her eyes now. But he went on:

'Janice! Who could harm a baby?'

'It didn't come to any harm. The police

found it half-a-mile away.'

Alan felt himself gaping stupidly. His jaw hung open, slack.

'The police told me — ' He stopped and remembered what they had said. 'They didn't tell me it had been found.'

Janice patted the bed. 'Come and have an hour with me.'

'No! *No!*'

She scowled, and he stumbled away.

'Where are you going, Alan?'

'To find Ruane!'

'Who's Ruane? Alan!' she shouted, and there was an iron edge to her voice that sent him running from the house.

If he had stayed, she would have turned those smoke-filled, spinning eyes on him, and his mind would have bent to her will. She could make him believe anything.

Ruane wasn't in the transport café.

# 13

Mersey Pagnall was a town of about thirty thousand inhabitants, but none of them was on the streets in the morning sunshine. The centre was deserted. Where did the derelicts go in the daytime?

Ruane was the only lifeline he had. And now, at seven on a fine June morning, he had no way of contacting him.

The proprietor of the transport café had been unhelpful. He knew Ruane only as a casual customer. He couldn't or wouldn't speculate on Ruane's whereabouts or whether or not he might have a settled home in the area.

Under normal circumstances, Alan would have turned to the police. But that wasn't to be thought of, not yet. It could be a ghastly mistake.

Alan Charnock groaned in indecision. It was his duty to contact the police. But Janice had said that the baby had been found, unharmed. Restless and trembling, Alan drove about the deserted streets, checking each doorway, scanning each public place, trying to drive the contrary voices from his head. Janice's sly smile haunted him. If he had stayed only a moment or two longer, she might have drowned him with her basilisk's stare. He shuddered.

What had kept her from harming him?

Some remnant of affection of six years of happy married life? Or was there another, unguessed, reason?

To drown the voices, Alan reached for the push-button on the car radio. Pop music blasted crazily until his head was ringing with the pleas of the singers.

He almost missed the local news broadcast.

' . . . no developments in the Harold Allison case, but latest reports from the hospital where Harold was taken last night suggest that he might not have suffered any permanent injury. It was thought at first that Harold, the Mersey Pagnall baby taken from his pram last night, might have suffered some spinal damage, but his own doctor says that

Harold's congenital spastic condition may have misled the doctors who first examined him. Mr. and Mrs. Allison waited at the hospital all night, and Mrs. Allison was given a sedative. So far there are no reports of a suspect in the case, though police are following up various pieces of information given by members of the public . . . '

'She wasn't lying,' said Alan. 'Christ, it's true!'

The baby was alive and well.

Who had taken it? Kids, Alan suggested. An impulse by some lonely teenage girl, who realized at once that she had done the wrong thing and then left the baby where it could be found. But speculation was unimportant. His wife had told him the truth. His suspicions were unfounded!

But the other things remained.

Alan stopped the car.

He groaned again in confusion. It had been the same pattern of events since the night of the séance. First the suspicions, then the grim evidence to confirm the suspicions. And, afterwards, the doubt.

Now, because he had heard the news of the baby's recovery, he was beginning to explain away the rest.

Soon, he knew, he would have deceived himself.

'But I saw her,' he cried aloud. 'I saw the mark on her! I saw her at Mrs. Worrall's!'

*Ruane.*

He had to find Ruane, for the red-faced wreck of a man had made some kind of sense of it all. Ruane was the only lifeline he had. The only person in the world he could turn to was an ex-priest, discredited and alcoholic!

*Alcoholic!*

He realized where he would find Ruane. In some pub or other. But first, it seemed overwhelmingly important that he should find out what had happened to Janice's victims.

He rang the Vicarage and heard a polite little voice ask who was speaking. The child brought its mother to the phone:

'Mr. Charnock?'

'Yes. I wanted a word with Mr. Unthank.'

'I'm sorry to say that the Vicar is not available at present.' He could feel the hostility in her.

'Is he all right?'

'I beg your pardon?' the woman said icily.

'I thought he might want to speak to me about my wife.'

'I'm sure I don't see any reason for it.'

'But last night — '

'Last night the Vicar became very ill. Very ill indeed!'

'What's the matter — '

'I can't discuss the state of his health with you, Mr. Charnock.'

'If you could ask him — '

'I'm afraid he isn't taking calls at the moment. Good morning, Mr. Charnock.'

It hadn't been a hallucination. It was more than ever essential to find Ruane.

Impatiently, Alan drove from one pub to another looking over the customers without seeing Ruane, then returned to the sleazy pub where he had seen Ruane the night before.

He asked the barman if he remembered seeing Ruane the night before, describing him in detail. The barman shook his head.

'He might have been here before. He's always in the pubs.'

The barman grinned.

'So's a lot of fellers.'

Alan made the rounds of the market pubs. There were nine of them. He drank tonic water, tomato juice, and more tonic water. No one knew Ruane by name. One or two customers thought they recognized him from Alan's description, but their pointed looks at empty glasses gave the lie to their recollections.

It wasn't till after two o'clock that Alan thought of the first time he had seen Ruane. He could see Janice's hate-filled eyes as she stared at him. Janice had known then, just as Ruane had known, that they were enemies.

The 'Coach and Horses' lay on the outskirts of Mersey Pagnall, a large and modern public-house with some pretensions to gentility.

He parked the Rover and half-ran to the Lounge Bar. The landlord looked at him.

'Do you remember a man called Ruane?' Alan asked. 'He was in here nearly four weeks ago. Middle-aged and in a shabby suit. He's big and heavy, with a red face. I was here with my wife and he spilled sherry — '

'Him?' the landlord pointed to a figure emerging from the toilet.

'Ruane!' called Alan. 'Ruane!'

The man lurched towards him.

'If he's a friend of yours, get him away, will you,' said the landlord. 'He's the kind I can do without.'

Alan stepped forward. Ruane was hopelessly drunk. There was no recognition in his eyes.

Ruane knew only that someone stood in his path. Stupidly he side-stepped, swaying and stumbling towards the bright sunshine at the open door.

Alan Charnock watched the shambling hulk that was Ruane. This, *this*, to counter the monster from the void?

Ruane shambled across the car park, somehow avoiding the concrete pillars set into the ground. Alan called to him:

'Ruane!'

He stopped and turned slowly. His face was swollen, redder than before. His eyes sunk deep into folds of fat. They peered without intelligence.

'Ruane, you're too drunk to know what I'm saying, but I'll say it.' Ruane swayed. 'You knew what it was when you saw the mark on Janice's hand — and you're going to tell me what I can do about it when you can talk. You're coming in the car and you're going to get sobered up. And then you're going to tell me what to do.' Alan choked back the self-pitying sobs that welled up inside him. 'Because if someone doesn't tell me what to do soon, I'm finished, Ruane, finished! I can't go to the police and I can't stay with her — don't you see, Ruane, I can't live with it!'

Something stirred in the alcoholic's mind, an echo of the past:

' . . . don't think of the sin, think of repentance . . . '

And he raised a hand in a sign that might have been meant to indicate mercy, pity and forgiveness.

'Into the car,' said Alan gently.

Ruane allowed himself to be steered towards the Rover. He fell asleep as soon as his great limbs and heavy torso were comfortably disposed.

Alan drove out of Mersey Pagnall towards the hills.

The day was now hot, June weather at last. Hundreds of picnickers were out, scrambling over the rocks and paddling in the streams. Alan had often brought Janice to the Peak National Park on days like this.

He left the windows of the car open and waited. A curious calm had come over him since finding Ruane.

Ruane lay snoring, his mouth open to reveal large nicotine-stained teeth. As the hours of stunning sunlight passed, Alan felt his own bodily condition improving.

The ulcer no longer attacked him. The headache subsided into a nagging, background reminder of the night's excesses. If he could have taken a shower and shaved, he would have felt fit and well.

At about six o'clock. Ruane stirred.

'Ruane,' said Alan.

The man's face turned blindly towards

the source of sound. The sunlight dazed him. He grunted and tried to stretch himself.

'Ruane, it's Alan Charnock.'

'Who?'

'Charnock! Last night in the transport café — don't you remember!'

Alan felt panic rising, for there was no intelligence in the broad, red face. The man was a hulk.

'You told me my wife is possessed. You said it would get worse. Ruane, I've been through hell these past four weeks!'

Ruane surfaced and knew that, at last, he must face the Enemy. He saw the fear and doubt in the white face.

'In Hell?'

'I spent the day looking for you — you were right, Ruane, I know that now.'

There were reserves of strength in the overweight body. Ruane heard the rising note in the young man's voice. He shrugged off the debilitating effects of the hours of drinking.

'You've suffered,' Ruane said. 'But you've not been in Hell. Not many unfortunates get a glimpse of the damnation ahead. I used to think I had when my little world blew up, but I was wrong.' His voice was strong and resonant now with the brogue coming through. He shifted, and Alan caught the stink of stale beer on his breath. 'No, we haven't seen Hell. We might, though.'

Ruane's deep voice was like a knell of doom.

'Might?'

Ruane felt as though a great weight had slipped onto his shoulders. 'When you seek out the Enemy, you must expect to do it in his own territory. Don't you know what you're asking me to do?'

'I thought you could get Janice to see what's happening to her. Can't you — what is it — exorcize this thing?'

'What thing?' Ruane asked.

'This Kelipoth — you told me last night you knew it for a kind of spirit And I read about things of that sort in a book on the occult. Surely you have some ideas about getting rid of it?'

Ruane felt dry. He needed to be rehydrated.

'So you want to try an exorcism, is that

it? But I'm not a priest.'

'But you were in orders!'

'Once a priest, always a priest, is that what you think?'

'Isn't it true in the Catholic Church?'

Ruane licked his lips. He thought of the bright robes, the incense, the haunting voices rising high into ancient arches; and the mystery of the Mass.

'I was relieved of my parochial duties,' he said, 'but you're right about it just the same. In the most extreme cases a priest must do his holy office, though he has shown himself unfit for the care of the parish.'

'Then you'll see her?'

Ruane's nerve-endings crawled.

'I need a drink.'

'No!'

Ruane saw the haggard face and in it some of his own spiritual exhaustion.

'No,' he agreed. 'No drink.'

# 14

After all, they had to find food and drink. Alan caught himself suggesting that they go back to his home, and then realized what he was saying. He stopped.

'No,' said Ruane. 'Not yet. There'll be a time when I must see her, but not for a while.'

'I have to go back sometime.'

'Leave that for the moment,' said Ruane.

They settled on a motorway café, and the long interrogation began.

Alan began to realize Ruane's quality as soon as he was into his story. The ex-priest's questions were freshly illuminating to his own memories of the bizarre sequence of events that had brought him such torment and horror.

'Did Mrs. Pierce get in touch with the medium after your wife forced the address out of her?'

'I don't know, but she's dead, isn't she?'

'So you guess that Mrs. Pierce knew what was happening to your wife?'

Alan thought of the woman's strained, blank face; and of Janice's wild eyes.

'Yes.'

'Get back to the séance. Who else saw the manifestation?'

'I don't know. At the time I put it down to a hallucination. But I did see it, and it was exactly the same at Mrs. Worrall's!'

'And its words?'

'I got the feeling it wanted to tell Janice something vital, but it couldn't get through. Not until the end, when she started to say she knew what it wanted — as though she had suddenly learned its language.'

'The gift of tongues,' said Ruane slowly. 'It is the same for the Damned too.'

'She had the mark,' said Alan. 'The mark that went.' He looked haggard.

Ruane went on quickly: 'That night, after the séance — there was an unusual degree of sexual activity?'

'Yes. Jerry Hood — one of the partners at the office — said the séance was responsible.'

'Yes,' said Ruane. 'First it marked your wife with the sign of the Beast. It needed a highly emotional state so that it could worm its way into your wife's soul, hence your wife's excited state. It begins with perverting the natural instincts, bringing a sense of depravity through unnatural lust. And then it could make the next advance.'

What had been guesswork became a logical progression.

'Sacrifice,' said Alan. 'Is that it?'

'Yes. The earliest form of sacrifice was that of the body's functions. Sexual intercourse is always associated with the early stages of devilry. She would have no need of the mark after that first night. Your wife would know herself as belonging to the monster.'

'Unthank had no chance against her,' he said. 'Had he?'

'He was taken unawares,' said Ruane. 'I don't know him, but I can see how it would happen.'

There was a long silence.

'She can make things disappear,' said Alan at last. He described the morning when he had awoken early and found the newspaper-wrapped package.

'Her nails were broken, and her hands had broken blisters. She has smooth white hands — '

'I saw them. Calm yourself!'

'She made me look down and there was no sign of damage to her hands!'

'It's a potent monster,' said Ruane. 'I've no doubt that by now she has developed stronger powers than self-healing.'

'But what had she been doing to get into that state?'

'It needed the magic of the grave. Things that had known life.'

Fear crawled inside Alan Charnock.

'Her hands? The grave?'

'If we were to examine the graveyards about here, we should find one that had been desecrated. It would be the grave of a young child — '

'No!'

'You have to know.' Ruane sighed as he felt the mysterious and profound authority that had once been his by right of office. 'There is worse.'

'But I can't take any more,' whispered Alan.

'Think of what your wife is suffering. You think you've looked into Hell. Where is her soul now?'

Alan Charnock's mind swam. Life collapsed inwards, suffocating him. Only the dread and the dark remained.

'You've been through enough for one day,' Ruane said to him and the words boomed grotesquely loud in Alan's head. 'It's time we went.'

Alan surfaced as Ruane got to his feet. 'Where to?'

'The Evil chose a pathway into this world. It may have left the marks of its coming. Please take me to the house of the medium, Mrs. Worrall.'

# 15

Repeated knocking brought no response. Ruane put his mouth to the letterbox:

'Mrs. Worrall! Are you there? I'd like one word with you! It would be a great favour, Mrs. Worrall.'

They waited.

'There's no one in,' said Alan. 'It's hopeless.'

'Wait,' said Ruane. He had noticed what Alan had missed. The heavy curtain of the front parlour had moved.

'Mrs. Worrall, it would be a kindness to open the door and let us in,' said Ruane. 'Will you, now?'

Slowly the curtain was pushed aside.

Alan took a step back, dread seizing his heart with a cold dankness. The negress's face was leprous. Blotched white and grey, the wide features had shrunk to those of an old woman.

She stared at Ruane and found something to reassure her. She nodded and the curtain fell back. A minute later, the two men heard shuffling steps. The door swung open.

'No one comes here,' she whispered. 'Not now.'

'You've been ill, Mrs. Worrall,' said Ruane. 'I can see you're not yourself. This won't take long. Can we come in?'

Her arms and legs were brittle sticks. Her eyes looked out from grey-white pits. Alan hardly recognized in her the robust, cheerful woman of four weeks ago.

'Is it about the hospital?' she asked. 'I don't want to go into hospital.'

She led the way into the parlour. Alan fancied he saw a stain on the green wallpaper where Janice had hurled the graveyard scavengings. He shuddered at his memories.

'The District Nurse said I was to go into hospital. But I don't want to leave my home.'

'We've come about Janice, my wife. She came to see you a couple of weeks ago, maybe a bit more. She often came,' said Alan.

The woman's sunken face turned to him.

She screamed.

Ruane proved his expertise.

'Outside,' he said to Alan. 'Wait outside!'

Alan moved without reluctance. He heard the woman's whimpering and Ruane's deep bass, very soothing, talking about loneliness and the ways of hospitals, about illnesses that come suddenly, and then about the way she lived.

There was much skill in the subtle transitions he made. Before she knew it, she was talking about her gift, and, within fifteen minutes, she could bring herself to mention Janice Charnock.

'You'd only known goodness from your spirit guides, Mrs. Worrall,' Ruane said. 'Little messages and a lot of comfort for the lonely. Never anything that frightened you before.'

'Never. When I was communicating, I was always in a dream, sir.'

'And you never remembered anything afterwards? That would be the way of a person with your power.'

'Only a feeling of peace. And sometimes I heard music and then afterwards I knew it was a hymn, but never the words.'

'But you remembered the spirit that night.'

She didn't answer for some time. Then Alan heard:

'I lost my gift. My friends called again and again, but I had to tell them that my powers were gone!' There was anger and fear in the way she complained, like a child reporting an injury by a vindictive and unforgiving bully who must find out.

'So the evil one destroyed your gift?'

'I told her! She wouldn't believe me, but I told her! It tore at me — look at me now! I didn't want the doctor and the nurse to come, but my friends said how I was, and now they want me to go into hospital. But I'm not sick!'

Alan shivered. Her illness would not be long-lasting. The medical authorities wanted her to die in reasonable dignity, not alone and afraid.

'You're very brave,' said Ruane.

'You are a man of God?'

'I think so.'

'Maybe you would pray with me?'

'Yes,' Ruane said, after a while. 'I will pray with you.'

The simple words rustled through the room. As they went from prayer to psalm and back to prayer, the woman's voice grew stronger. It took on the richness of her people's deep-rooted beliefs, spreading calmness and hope through Alan's mind.

Again time passed in silence.

'Why have you come to me?' Mrs. Worrall asked quite calmly

'The man with me is the husband of the blonde woman. The pale, slim woman who has the evil in her soul. May I bring him to you?'

'Yes.'

'You can come in now, Alan,' called Ruane.

'Mrs. Worrall, we brought this sadness and distress,' said Alan.

'Sit down, sir,' she told him. 'Just tell me what I can do. I know you want something, and I know you are both good men.' To Alan she said: 'I was afraid at first, but now I am not.'

'Thank you,' said Alan. 'I want to destroy this thing that holds my poor wife.'

The woman shivered. 'It's too strong!'

'Maybe,' said Ruane. 'But there is nothing in creation that can withstand the majesty and power of Almighty God. That we must all believe, with all our hearts.'

She gained renewed courage. 'I have said I will do what you ask.'

Ruane got to his feet.

'I want you to go into a trance. I know you said you'd lost your powers, but I have some ability in your own practices,' he said. 'Mrs. Worrall, don't be offended if I say that all mediums rely on a kind of hypnosis, and usually they can induce it themselves. Will you let me help you to go into a trance?'

Alan Charnock wondered at the transformation in the ex-priest. There was a solemn dignity in all his movements. He no longer shambled as he moved. His broad back was straighter, his demeanor that of a man who is certain of himself.

But Alan could not let him raise the terrible monster again. He had seen the sheer, mind-rending terror of the woman before.

'You can't ask her to do it!' he said harshly. 'Ruane, I've seen it.'

Ruane spoke in a low voice: 'Mrs. Worrall, are you afraid?'

She nodded. Her slack lips trembled.

'But you trust in the everlasting mercy of God?'

Her grey-lined eyes cleared and she looked at Alan Charnock:

'If I can do this, I will. I have to help you, and soon.'

Alan realized that she knew she was near the end of her life. He turned to Ruane, but the ex-priest stopped him with a gesture. To Mrs. Worrall he said:

'Sit in that chair, facing me. Rest easy. Think of peace. Think of your kind friends. Let your hands lie in your lap. And look at me all the time.'

'Yes.' She watched Ruane with a blind and helpless trust.

Minutes burned away. Through Alan Charnock's mind flickered the images from another, grimmer visit to the room. He saw again the weird cabbalistic markings as his wife's swaying body built up hypnotic evil patterns. They were the imprint of the monster, released from its howling abyss to gouge into Janice's soul.

Mrs. Worrall's eyes glazed. Her mouth opened. She began to sing, in a tiny, lost voice the hymn that had begun the séance at the Spiritualist hall.

'Sleep,' said Ruane, when she had finished.

At once her eyes closed and her breathing became low, regular and shallow.

Alan shivered.

'You'll kill her, Ruane — you can't bring the devil down to — '

'Quiet. I can't and I won't call on the Evil One. Alan, you have to believe in what I say!'

'Then why put her into a trance?'

'I want to speak to the mind below the level of everyday memory. She will have residual memories of what passed during the sessions with your wife. There will be memories, and words too, perhaps. Not of this thing, this evil monster, but of what your wife said to it. You agree that I may ask her?'

'Is there any danger to her?'

'Some. She could awaken prematurely and then, in her poor physical condition, there could be a reaction of deep shock.'

'Is there much chance of her awakening?'

'Not if I probe carefully. I studied under a leading authority as a young man.'

'But — '

'Look, I'm not thinking of your wife only. You said there was another woman with your wife. It could spread, this vileness.'

'Spread?'

Ruane waved him to silence. The time was now.

'Mrs. Worrall?' he said.

'Who are you?' she murmured.

'A friend. I want to ask you about Janice Charnock. She came to you, didn't she?'

There was a momentary spasm that worked its way through her whole body.

Ruane waited. The woman sat blindly,

her hands not trembling. 'Mrs. Worrall, Janice was marked on the hand.'

'Yes.'

'Why?'

'She told me it was the sign that she was chosen. When she knew that, the mark went.'

'She harmed you badly.'

'Not her!' the woman called immediately. 'No, not her!'

'Mrs. Worrall, what did Janice want from you?'

'She hurt me!' whimpered the grey-faced negress. 'Oh, she tore my heart.'

'To find out something?'

'Yes! She had to find out the Way!'

'And did she?'

'She ripped me so bad, I couldn't see in the dark — I felt blood all around, blood and death, and I had to let go!'

She was crying out now in helpless fright, but Ruane persisted.

'There is a Way for her to follow?'

'Yes! Blood!'

'What blood?'

'The small dog only kept it quiet for a few days, don't you see?' Her blind, shuttered eyes turned from Ruane to a corner. Alan's spine chilled. There was no shadowy horror, but she thought there was.

'What must she do now?' said Ruane.

'It must have the power,' she answered. 'It must have blood. The dead child made it worse. There has to be life. There must be living blood.'

'Blood,' whispered Alan Charnock. He felt himself reeling. 'A dead child!'

Ruane hissed: 'Be silent! See, she wants to speak!'

The medium struggled for her words, as if they were so impatient for utterance that there was no proper order amongst them:

'The Way — she knows! And the Place of Sacrifice! Oh, she told me the Place where the night is alive and the blood runs red and strong!'

'What Place!' called Ruane. 'The Way is through blood — we know that, but where — where is the Place, Mrs. Worrall?'

'Dark and high stones! Dark and a black rock! Night and the scent of blood!

Where the high stones form a ring!'

'Dear God, it's a prescient vision!' whispered Ruane. 'She can see an ancient place of sacrifice.'

'And Janice?' breathed Alan.

'Where — tell me a name for the Place, Mrs. Worrall,' Ruane ordered. 'Just a name and then we trouble you no more, dear sister. A name!'

'Kelipoth!'

'No!' roared Ruane suddenly. 'Not the Name of the Damned! Tell me the name of the Place of Sacrifice, Mrs. Worrall! Tell me!'

The woman jerked epileptically. Alan Charnock might have felt pity for her but for the sudden appalling coldness of the room. The temperature went down so quickly that he felt as though he had plunged into freezing fog. Mist shrouded the corner where the apparition had formed. He knew the thing was near.

Ruane sensed the danger. 'The name!' he roared.

The thing was very near now. Its terrible Presence affected all three of them. But Ruane was relentless.

'Tell it!' he roared commandingly.

'It rips my heart!'

'You must tell!'

Alan saw the comer of the room begin to fill with the tiny white motes that had preceded the manifestation in the Spiritualist hall.

There was a sullen, threatening silence. The room glistened with frost, stark white frost, and the monstrous thing began to have definition.

Into the silence, the medium's voice trembled:

'Shinlaw! The rocks of Shinlaw! On the night of the no dark, it must be Blood!'

Ruane raised his hands and rapidly intoned:

'O Lord and Holy Father, O Blessed Mother of God, O Sweet Jesus, command that the Evil that is Present be utterly Confounded! Give thy Servants Relief from all Evil that Troubles them, and grant that the Worm that Dieth not be Sent to the Pit from which it Came!'

He made the sign of the Cross and called again:

'In the Name of the Lord Jesus, begone!'

The eerie half-solid beginnings of a shape held still.

'I command thee. *Begone*!' roared Ruane.

The frail woman opened her eyes. And the shape merged with the soft shadows in the corner. In a few seconds, it might never have been.

'Too much power,' Ruane said. 'It has a furious and awful Power!'

# 16

The cold and coiled Evil had gone, the freezing whiteness with it. Mrs. Worrall looked tired but relaxed, almost happy.

'Did you talk to my Golden Girl? Did she come?'

'No, Mrs. Worrall, but don't be disappointed. We learned what we came for. Is your mind clearer now?'

Ruane had asked the right question.

'The vibrations were good,' she said. 'My Golden Girl has gone, but I know I shall not be parted from her for long.'

'Go into hospital, as your doctor says,' Ruane advised.

'If you say it is right, sir.'

She accepted it. Again, Alan was conscious of Ruane's new-found confidence. Alan said, suddenly hopeful:

'She will get better now?'

'No. I can't reverse the harm done to her, nor can any man.' Ruane looked tired and dispirited. 'This evil is hideously strong. It can destroy us all.'

Ruane closed his eyes. The Thing had got to him, chill and terrible. His nerve-endings crawled with the need for alcohol. Anything, but preferably whisky. A few drinks, five minutes for it to surge through the bloodstream, and then forgetfulness, no more of the ravening, mindless Evil.

'But she looked better after you put her in the trance — much better! You could try the same thing with Janice, couldn't you?'

'So you still think I can exorcize this devil?'

His almost cynical tone dismayed Alan.

'Yes!' It had to be yes. Otherwise, what was there?

Ruane shook his head.

'You've seen what it can do. That poor woman is not long for this world. Think of what it can do to you. And to me.'

'You're giving up?' Alan was incredulous. 'You're saying nothing can be done for Jan!'

'Not by me.' Ruane licked his lips. He thought of the malt sparkle of a glass of whisky, amber through diamonds.

'But you said you'd help me! Why, you bastard, you just want to get back on the bottle! You do, Ruane!' Alan snarled in his rage. 'You're as bad as Unthank — you're just as weak as that poor wretch! I thought you could smell out evil! You told me you knew what to do! And you do! You're scared, you drunken bastard! Scared and weak, Ruane! We know where to find it — we know where it will be! *Why can't you face it! Why can't you tackle it! You know you should!*'

Ruane tried to retreat into a private world.

He had thought he could get away from it. Away from the helpless and furious cry in the night. Away from the blank horror in the medium's blind face as she stared into a dark corner; away from this terror-stricken young man whose life had been peaceful, humdrum, and uneventful until the husk from the Pit had crawled into his wife's mind.

'All right!' Ruane rasped. He fought down the trembling need that affected his whole body, denying it hope. *No alcohol.*

Not one drink. That was the way they did it in the alcoholics' self-help clubs. *Not one drink!* Cold turkey. Face it, tackle it, stand up to it. Just as Charnock had done. A naive and weak young man, he had yet shown resource. He had been afraid, but he was not feeble. Unprepared, without knowledge, he had faced the Enemy. Alone.

Without thinking about his answer, Ruane said:

'I'm sorry. I won't fail you. I always knew I had to fight this thing. You won't be alone.' He found his mind clearing. 'I heard it shout in the night,' he said. 'I heard it cry out, and I believe it challenged me even then. It knew someone would hear.'

Alan Charnock sighed. Ruane had committed himself.

'Then you'll exorcize it?'

Ruane shook his head.

'It's too strong for me as I am now. You know what it can do, and so do I. And don't look at me like that! This thing isn't an ordinary poltergeist or an uneasy human spirit! Man, it's an unknown devil

— it's the worst of all, because it hasn't known what life is. It's part of the debris of the universe. It's something apart from what God made. It's the ultimate Enemy because it can't possibly be understood by man!'

Alan began to realize the magnitude of his request.

'Well?'

'You know, man, it's an impossible thing you're asking me to do. Alan, our Lord Himself had to send such a one into the bodies of pigs and drown them by the thousand to rid the land of its Power!'

' "My name is legion",' whispered Alan.

'It's name is Kelipoth! Husk of evil, shell of vileness, demon or devil that wants life because it has never known life!'

Alan shuddered.

'Mrs. Worrall. The night of the séance. I remember now. Her spirit guide warned of the life-that-is-not-life.' He remembered the evil-smelling dankness. 'It was near?'

'Too near,' said Ruane.

'If you won't exorcize it what can I do?

I can't go to the police. If I could, what would I say? What would they do?' He felt self-pity welling up inside him. 'You don't know Janice! She wasn't perfect, but when we were together, everything was right! And when she smiled at me, I — '

He couldn't say the tender thing he felt.

'How could I report her to the police?'

'No police, Alan. No police, just as I can't go to my authorities. If I asked my former Bishop for help, he'd order me not to interfere.' Ruane laughed without mirth. 'He'd take it for drunken boasting. He'd tell me I'd come to him simply to try to get back my parish.'

They looked at each other. Each saw weakness.

In Ruane, Alan sensed the desolation of the man who has chosen a path for himself and then stepped aside from it. It was a difficult and demanding path, and Ruane's fall had brought a correspondingly hurtful shame. Ruane suffered Alan's almost hopeless stare, and, in turn, watched a weak man try to find, somewhere, the strength he needed.

It was Alan who spoke first.

'Mrs. Worrall said the place was Shinlaw. On the night of no dark. And blood. Ruane, that will be when it begins to live.'

'Yes.'

'I'll find that place — Shinlaw.'

Ruane nodded. Charnock had gained a kind of fortitude from his tormented helplessness.

'The night of no dark,' Alan went on. 'It doesn't make sense. But I can watch her. And wait. It will be in the hills. I'll look on an Ordnance Survey map.' He looked at the elaborate console of the Rover. It had once given him pleasure. 'It's my job,' he said to Ruane. 'I know about places. I'll find Shinlaw. She said it was a circle of rocks. It'll be on the maps.'

Ruane could have wept for him.

'And when you've found it?'

Alan's voice was low.

'I can't let her — I can't just stand by. She's my *wife!*'

Ruane clenched his hands. Charnock was, after all, one of those subdued, quiescent spirits that might remain unknown to the grave; but, if the need arose, they emerged like a chrysalis to force and fight, to action and fury.

And it was all useless effort. The thing would conquer.

The passion and the brief fury of a weak man made strong by evil times were not enough, not for this horror. Ruane had known evil, but never anything remotely approaching the thing that possessed Alan Charnock's wife.

And he, Ruane, was all that stood between this trembling, hopeless, but undaunted young man and the Pit. And what was he, Ruane? What could he do?

No drink. That was a start. Ruane swore it, solemnly and slowly.

'Alan,' he said, as a clarity of purpose came to him. 'I can't go to my Bishop. But I know a man who can advise us. He'll see me, I think. He knows about the things from the abyss. He's served abroad in Africa and in Asia. I won't tell you his name, but he's one of the few men who write on parapsychology who are listened to by both scientists and churchmen.'

'A priest?' and Alan knew he sounded bitter.

'No,' said Ruane. 'More. Truly, Alan. He lived a full life and then chose to go into a closed Order. He has seen more of the evil of this world than any man. I met him only once.' Ruane felt the weight of his own spiritual failure. 'When I — When I — When I left the Church,' he said strongly, 'he was the only one who wrote to me.'

'And?'

'He said he was my friend.'

'What do I do?' Alan asked.

'Go back to your wife. So far, she hasn't attempted to influence you, has she?'

'No.'

'She won't.'

'I read something about these spirits — '

'Don't. Don't read any more, don't attempt to learn what you can never understand. Don't even think of challenging the ghoul that has possession of your wife's soul. Not by a single word, not by a glance or a casual look! Let me consult this expert and then we will decide what is to be done.'

'How long will it take?'

'I can get a train to London tomorrow morning. I should be back in the evening.'

'Then?'

'I'll telephone.'

'I'll be at home.' Alan took in the decrepit clothes. 'You'll need money.' He took a small wad of notes from his wallet.

Ruane stamped down speculation on the days of oblivion it would pay for. He took it and saw doubt in Alan Charnock's face.

'I'll ring,' he said. 'I won't fail you. Now go home. Watch and learn but never question. I'll try to find out what kind of demon we must send back to the Pit.'

Alan Charnock drove off and tried to keep the knowledge in a tight-locked compartment of his mind.

He raced the engine of the Rover to announce his arrival before switching off. In the gloom of the warm June evening, he could see the glow of the pink-shaded lights. Janice was in the lounge.

It took a full minute to summon the nerve to open the front door. He paused, tense yet flaccid, sinews like iron thread through gelatine.

And then Janice was in front of him.

'Jan!'

She had appeared like a wraith. Terror ripped through him. Ruane had said she would have new powers —

'Shut the door, Alan,' she said, and she was precise, neat, blonde Janice, not a wraith, because the door of the lounge was open behind her, and she had come through it.

*Be normal*, Ruane had told him. *Normal!*

'I'm sorry I didn't ring to say I'd be out last night! I didn't want you to be worried. And coming back, the car broke — '

'Coming back from where?'

She wasn't especially angry. After a night and a day of absence, unexplained absence.

'My uncle's! In Gloucester! He was taken ill — I got a phone call.' There was an uncle. 'He was very ill, Jan. You know how it is when there aren't any phones — '

'Not just now,' said Janice. 'I've a few friends round for coffee.'

'Friends?'

Janice smiled, and Alan knew he could never be free of the terror the smile brought. Her white face was drawn, as haggard as he knew his own to be. Now, when she smiled, the long teeth at the side of her mouth, and her pointed chin, gave her face the sharpness of a medieval grotesque.

'Friends?' repeated Alan, for she made no sign to move nor to answer.

'See,' she said, moving at last.

Alan stepped forward with the heavy tread of a sleepwalker. He looked into the lounge.

There were seven or eight of them, women he knew, some only vaguely. Myra Bentley, with her bright eyes and the same sharp-toothed smile that slit his wife's face. The Baines-Ogden woman, massively antagonistic. And she had been so furious about the terrier. Now she was one with Janice. A woman he knew only as Brenda. An older woman, forty at least, who ran a small boutique. More of them, but all staring back at him, all with that thin, razor-edged smile.

*The infection could spread.* So Ruane had said. It had.

Alan felt himself sinking into darkness. But he was still on his feet, somehow in possession of his faculties. He was lost in a fog of horror, yet able to speak and know what he said.

'Jan?'

'Yes, Alan?'

He knew it was madness, but he said it.

'Mr. Unthank isn't taking any calls.' It was the hint of a challenge. 'His wife says he's ill.'

Cursing himself for ignoring Ruane's warning, Alan tried to call back the useless words. He couldn't look at Janice, not into her eyes. Instead, he pivoted and half-stepped to the door-frame of the lounge. There were more than eight of them. And their mad, whirling eyes gleamed back at him, every woman silent and hostile and utterly terrifying.

Myra Bentley was the worst. Like a rabbit seeking to evade a ferret's red stare, Alan moved his neck but he could not look away from Myra. He saw past the basilisk glare and into the crazy, mote-filled emptiness. And Myra was giggling. Just as in the church.

Before he fell, someone gripped his shoulder. Janice was saying something:

'Alan's been ill!' she called, loud and imperious.

'Poor Alan!' giggled Myra. Her eyes glared.

'It's his ulcer,' said Janice, voice iron-edged.

'Poor Alan!' called the others,

He felt their gaze on his midriff.

Then an appalling agony hit him. A white-hot lance of torment slid into his abdomen, and he doubled up, shrieking soundlessly.

'No!' grated his wife. 'No more!'

Janice's grip was a steel claw to drag him upright and face the women again. Their eyes stopped spinning, the terrible redness faded, the black void fell away.

'He's better now!' Janice called. 'But he

190

might have a relapse. Had you better go to bed, Alan?'

He knew he had been the worst of fools. Simply, they could kill him. With a little concerted effort, hardly anything at all, they had projected a flash of pure agony through him.

'It might be his heart,' said Myra. 'Has he been doing too much? Has he a weak heart, Janice?'

She very much wanted to use her power.

'No!' spat Janice. 'It's just an ulcer. And he's going to be careful, aren't you, Alan?'

The Baines-Ogden woman began to mutter, but Janice stared her into silence. They all smiled, horrible fixed smiles.

'Aren't you, Alan!' rasped Janice.

'Yes!'

He stumbled as she pushed him towards the stairs. Janice followed. He let his clothes fall away. Janice watched like a tired and impatient nurse. He huddled under the duvet, heart beating erratically, thoughts racing about till they could find the hidden corner of the mind where they would huddle too.

'Curtains!' said Janice irately.

He looked as she stared at the long drapes on the other side of the room. She appeared to concentrate. Three, four seconds passed.

Alan Charnock felt the dankness of terror once more.

Unbelievably, the curtains slid smoothly and noiselessly together. Janice grinned secretly, as if guiltily proud of a trick newly learned, one not to be displayed, a very secret power.

'You don't want hot chocolate, do you, Alan?' she said gaily.

'No.'

'Then get some sleep. I may be late. *Sleep*!'

And he did sleep, without conscious effort and without any dreams of blood and darkness. His nervous exhaustion was complete.

It was eight on Monday morning when he awoke, and Janice was not in bed. After minutes, then an hour of careful listening, he searched the house.

His wife had gone to work.

# 17

'You look,' said Jerry Hood, 'like a skinned snake.' His ugly face was thoughtful. 'Booze? You shouldn't with your guts. Not — You've not been playing ghosties again with the lovely Janice, have you? No more séances, Alan?'

The banter didn't worry Alan. He draped his desk with the maps.

'You have been overdoing it, my lad,' said Jerry. 'Anything wrong?'

'Nothing.'

'What are you looking for?'

Alan checked the grid reference.

'Shinlaw.'

'Village?'

'I doubt it.'

'Development area?'

'You could say that.'

'Something in it for us?'

'Could be.' What did it matter if he lied?

'Housing?'

'Quite possibly. I heard a whisper.'

'Shinlaw? Far from here?'

'In the hills.'

'Never heard of it . . . wait a minute!' Jerry's ugly faced creased in a smile.

He pointed to a map.

'*Scinlaw* not Shinlaw. There it is — but it's no go for development. Restricted. You couldn't build a kennel without a public inquiry. And then it'd have to be made of gritstone.'

'Thanks, Jerry.'

So it wasn't Shinlaw, but Scinlaw. From the contours it must be on a steepish hill. Alan knew the area. It was wilder and rougher than the tourist liked. In winter it was flayed by the prevailing winds and had a grim bleakness.

'Scinlaw,' thought Alan. 'Christ, I hope she won't go.' He had, nevertheless, something to tell Ruane.

If Ruane ever telephoned.

★　★　★

Alan drove into the hills in a dreamy daze. He couldn't believe that it was happening, that Janice meant to take the women on some diabolical Women's Institute outing. It was unbelievable.

The Rover ate up the miles. Lorries ground slowly up the winding roads, and then Alan left the traffic as he turned off into a minor road. There was no signpost. Scinlaw was unmarked.

He stopped at the side of an escarpment.

The sky was white-patched with drifting high cloud. Faint sheep cries came from the rocks above the road, then the sound of a grouse calling attention to his presence.

He took the map and climbed.

It took only a minute or two to orient himself. The escarpment gave a wide panoramic view of the moors. Mersey Pagnall lay south-east, twenty miles away. The smudge of smoke to the north was a manufacturing town famous for its footballers. Two narrow streams ahead, and almost due east, were tributaries of the Lune. The irregular, straggling rocks on the hill between the streams was Scinlaw.

He looked at his polished shoes and the marshy ground. A magpie swung past very low, its white plumage brilliant against the green bracken. Doubts ferreted around his mind.

It was impossible, Alan said to himself. The medium must be wrong. She had said Shinlaw, not Scinlaw. He looked at his map again, and then at the rocks. They formed a rough circle. In the middle was a vast rectangular slab, too regular in form to be natural. Alan shuddered and thought of the blood-blotched nightdress. They couldn't be intending to come here — not *here*, not a hideous sacrificial scene *here*?

Clouds obscured the sunlight, and the rocks grew dark. Heavy shadow dimmed the centre of the circle. The rocks looked like misshapen tombstones.

Alan could not will himself to inspect the dark circle. He retreated, stunned by thoughts he could not express.

He could not approach the grim, dark rocks, not alone.

★   ★   ★

Janice was late. Alan tried to read his newspaper, but the print blurred. When he switched on the television set, the pictures refused to match the words. He swallowed some bread and cheese and waited for the inevitable reaction from his ulcer. It was almost a relief when it came.

Ruane hadn't called.

Myra Bentley entered the house without knocking.

'Janice had to see some of the girls,' she called. 'How are you, Alan?'

The ulcer stabbed. Alan felt the cheese sour in his guts. He held the paper against her gaze, a ridiculous shield.

'Better,' he croaked.

She was so normal, so neighbourly, so nice. And she was a guard, a sentry, set to watch him.

'Janice shouldn't neglect you like this. Shall I make you some coffee?'

The phone rang. Alan froze, mind whirling.

'Aren't you going to answer it?'

'Yes. Yes!'

Myra smiled at him, a carefree and open smile. She watched him from the lounge door. It was Ruane.

Alan heard himself chattering like a frightened child:

'Where are you? I've been waiting for you to call, go ahead, what's happened? Have you anything worked out?' And Myra Bentley waited, relaxed and alert at the same time.

Ruane's voice was hoarse and urgent.

'Alan, something's wrong?'

'No.'

'Sure, man?'

Ruane listened for a moment.

'You're alone?'

'No.'

'Your wife?'

'No.'

'But you can't talk freely?'

'No.'

'Then listen.'

'Yes.'

'I couldn't see the man I told you about today. He was in retreat — it means he was meditating and they wouldn't let me disturb him. But I'm seeing him first thing tomorrow morning. It's vital meanwhile that you don't alarm your wife.

Don't give her any indication that you suspect her. Not by any sign — it's even more important than before. Do you understand that, Alan?'

Myra's smile had gone. Alan watched her, hypnotized.

'I've got it. I understand. Why?'

'Because I know what the medium meant when she said 'the night of no dark'. I should have worked it out before this.'

Alan thought of the griping pain, the sudden jolt of agony. Nevertheless, he kept his voice steady. 'I've got that.'

' 'The night of no dark' means what it implies — a night when it doesn't get dark. But that doesn't happen, except in more northerly parts of Europe — and the people who gave Shinlaw its name came from the far north! In the basic pennanic language, the word 'law' means a mound, usually a burial mound. And 'shin' can mean either shining, or something else. I was misled at first because I took 'shin' to have something to do with the idea of 'no dark'. I thought Shinlaw was 'the shining hill' or the 'bright hill'.'

'Well?' said Alan, thinking of the dark rocks.

'It doesn't.'

'No.'

'There's another word, 'Scinnan'.'

'I know. We had the wrong name.'

Myra's features were sharp, just as Janice's had been. Alan's hand shook on the phone.

'The wrong name,' agreed Ruane sombrely. ''Scinnan' is 'Devil'. 'Scinlaw' is 'The Devil's Mound'.'

'It would be,' said Alan.

'And the reason I don't want you to betray yourself is this. The 'night of no dark' in the northerly parts of Europe is just that. The night when the sun never sets. The longest night of all.'

Alan's gaze rested on a calendar. The figures would not make sense. 'Yes?'

'Tomorrow is the summer solstice. It's the longest day of the year. It was once a pagan festival and in later times witches' Sabbath. You must not on any account give your wife a warning that you know it! There is worse to come!'

Myra's eyes spun.

'Bad news, Alan?' she whispered harshly.

'Hello?' said Ruane.

Alan stood rock-still. Fire lanced through him. He could not answer Ruane.

'Alan?' breathed Myra. 'Who is it?'

'There's trouble?' said Ruane urgently. 'Listen! I'll find out what to do tomorrow morning, and I'll get the noon train back — I won't ring you again, but I'll meet you at the railway station in Mersey Pagnall. Be there on the hour, every hour from six tomorrow evening. Is that clear?'

Alan heard, but the words barely registered. Myra was holding him in her terrible stare, and the receiver was suddenly slime in his hand. He let it drop away as the crawling, decaying matter dripped from his hand. Then the wire became a living thing.

Jerking and writhing, it sent the body of the telephone hurtling through the air to smash solidly against an oak chest, jangling into silence.

Myra was still there. Her eyes were dark and empty now.

'Was it bad news?' she said, her voice iron-edged, harsh and demanding.

'No!'

'Who was it?'

'A friend.'

'Name?'

'Ruane.'

'And who's Ruane?'

Alan saw a way out.

'A drinking friend. I met him in a pub.'

'A drinking friend!' Myra was contemptuous. 'Janice said you'd been drinking a lot, Alan. Still, social drinking never harmed anyone, did it?'

She seemed satisfied with that.

When she had gone, Alan looked at the wire that had jerked like a living thing, at the receiver, which had been an evil-smelling goblet of slime. The telephone was shattered.

Myra could make things move too. How had things come to this?

The séance, innocuous at first. A joke. And then the grey shape that had come from some astral void to dominate his wife. A dog missing and then found torn. The Baines-Ogden woman, wildly furious at first and now a part of the evil. A dead child torn from its grave, and a living priest rutting in his own pulpit. Linda Pierce drawn under the massive wheels, and the medium blasted as if by fire. The women trying to kill him.

And now he was terrified into submission by a look from Myra Bentley. In his own house, he had capitulated when the evil glare caught him.

Ruane had said it would be worse the next day.

*Worse?*

Alan took four of the sleeping tablets and they worked.

In the morning, Janice had never been more charming.

She cooked a delicious breakfast. Her conversation was bright and animated. Alan, still sluggish from the effects of the sleeping tablets, replied in monosyllables to her chatter. She said he should not drive her to the shop, because he looked tired.

As she left, she said: 'Myra thought you looked worried last night, Alan.'

'Oh no,' he said quickly. 'I can't think

how she got that idea.' Play it cool, think of what Ruane said and hold on to that thought. *Cool it*.

'She said you'd had a distressing phone call. Someone called Ruane,'

'Ruane? Oh no.'

'Then nothing's worrying you?'

'No, Jan.'

'I'll be late again tonight.'

It was the longest day of the year. Involuntarily, Alan looked out and saw it would be a brilliant June day with a haze on the moors. The dark stones would retain their heat all night, warm to the touch, warm gritty stone and soft lichens.

'I said I'll be late tonight,' Janice repeated.

'I — ' He was going to say he knew.

'So you can get your own meal?'

'Yes, Jan.'

'I may be very late.'

'Oh?'

She stepped slowly across the kitchen. Then, to his amazement, she caressed him, very tenderly.

'But you're not the jealous sort, are

you? You wouldn't worry how late I was, would you?'

'I might,' he said, almost daring her.

Her face froze. 'It wouldn't do, Alan. It wouldn't do at all. You do see?'

He nodded. 'Yes, Jan.'

Then she kissed him.

'I do love you,' she whispered in a small and lonely voice.

His mind cried out in frustrated anger. Do nothing? *Do nothing*! But she was warning him, telling him not to try to stop her.

He said, bitterness welling up:

'And I love you, Jan! More than I can say!'

She smiled, dazzling as ever, almost innocent. But her eyes were fixed elsewhere. She was looking into a darkness where he would be lost, and she was alien and hostile to all humankind.

Alan watched her walk down the street. Really, it needed no discussion, not this time. If Ruane did not meet him, he would go alone. It was inevitable. He could not stand by and see her damned.

★ ★ ★

The station had once been important, but the new motorway had taken most of its business. There was only one person on duty, a small, rotund, middle-aged porter-cum-ticket collector who answered Alan's repeated questioning with unfailing patience. Three trains had come and gone. Ruane had not appeared.

Was there a delay on the London line? There wasn't. Had anyone left a message for Mr. Charnock? No. Was it possible that there would be a message at the mainline station? Mr. Charnock could ring through if he wished. Ruane hadn't left a message. By eight o'clock with the sun still white-bright, Alan's nerves were raw. He was full of energy, so much so that he could not keep still. Up and down the hot platform he walked, his nylon shirt clammy against the sweat, his mouth dry and his eyes hurting from the glare of concrete.

What would happen tonight? Tonight, when other terrible women were with her, adding their supplications to hers? What then?

Monstrous visions rose up in his mind. A long flat stone, grey-black and hot to the touch. And on it? *Blood and darkness*, the medium had said. Blood. And that primeval shape straining for birth.

The train slid in unnoticed.

Three people got out. Alan saw them and then the train. A fourth passenger left the green diesel coach.

'Ruane!' roared Alan.

⋆   ⋆   ⋆

Explanations took time.

Ruane's unnamed expert was a sick old man, his mind filled with peaceful visions. The abbot was reluctant to allow Ruane in at all, but he could not exclude him, not when Ruane showed him the letter he had kept in his wallet. It was undeniable. 'Come when you need me,' the words said. 'At any time.'

'Well?' Alan almost snarled.

'On his advice, I am to accompany you

to the meeting place.'

'Thank God!'

'For this much, yes, but wait till you hear the rest. How is it with you first? Man, you'll never last out if you go on like this — have you eaten?'

'I couldn't! We've got to get to Scinlaw — '

'Not yet. Not for some hours. We must prepare as well as we can. You can't face what we must face in that condition.'

'Tell me what you've been able to find out!'

Ruane hesitated. 'Then you'll eat?'

'Yes.'

'Sit here, in the shade.'

And so, in the deep shade of the rowans outside the station, Alan heard Ruane's instructions.

'There are ways of fighting demons, ways known to the Church since its earliest days. With fire — and we must prepare for that, Alan, and with holy water. I have a phial newly sanctified by a bishop. Fire and water, the primeval force of good. And this.' And Ruane drew out a crucifix.

'It is my own.'

The ivory and ebony had worn smooth by much handling. 'The rest is not for us. All the herbs and the sympathetic magic of paganism cannot help us. We must trust in the most direct methods, the basic powers.'

Alan touched the Cross.

'Fire?' He could not begin to imagine what Ruane meant.

'Tonight we have to burn the evil thing. And we must choose exactly the right moment!' The ex-priest's voice trembled.

'When?'

'We'll know. This is the vital factor, if we wish to save your wife, her friend too.'

'It's more than these,' said Alan. 'I counted twelve. And Janice.'

'So. Thirteen. A coven.' Ruane nodded. 'That is the magic number. But the most important factor is our timing — I have a rough idea of the kind of ritual it will be, and my friend has told me exactly when to intervene. There is a chance. We must seize it! There is one moment when they will be helpless.'

Alan could see the grey-black stone

again with a terrible vividness.

'I went to Scinlaw — '

'You shouldn't have! Did they see you?'

'No.'

'Thank God!'

'I spoke to Janice about Unthank.'

'Fool!' Ruane blazed at him. Then, with compassion, he said: 'Forgive me. It is your wife's soul.'

'They looked at me — ' shuddered Alan. 'They wanted to kill me. She stopped them. Myra Bentley said I had a weak heart, but Janice halted them!'

'Because she is still a human being!' cried Ruane. 'Because the thing is inside her, but it has not yet destroyed her! And this is why we have to choose exactly the right moment!'

'Is there a real possibility of saving her?' Alan felt hope rising once more.

Ruane was excited and almost confident. 'Yes! There has to be a sacrifice and then the evil spirit becomes all-powerful. But for a brief period, it is in a limbo between the Pit and this world. At the moment of sacrifice, the evil thing is helpless. It is suspended between life and the abyss, and if I can keep it at bay for long enough by the power of the crucifix and the Holy Water, then it cannot cross! If, in that few seconds, it can be held back, then it can be destroyed!'

Something troubled Alan. He realized what it was.

'Sacrifice? What kind of sacrifice?'

'My friend wasn't sure what form it would take,' said Ruane. 'The body's lust first — you know how it happened to you. There will be sexual release. Then there must be blood, perhaps that of a small animal.' He frowned. 'He told me of the worst vileness. Of young children offered to the Devil. It happened in Europe even as late as the eighteenth century. And in Africa it is still known.'

'But Janice wouldn't hurt a baby!' Alan burst out in relief. 'I thought — There was a child missing, Ruane, but it was discovered soon afterwards unharmed. I had this crazy idea on Saturday night that Janice and Myra had taken this spastic child from its pram — '

'Here?' Ruane gripped Alan's arm. 'In the town?'

'Yes. It wasn't harmed.'

Ruane's face hardened.

'No,' he said. 'It was not fit. It was no sacrifice. This is far worse than I imagined!'

'Why? It can't be! There's nothing in — '

'A spastic child, don't you see! Deformed! A sacrifice must be perfect! Perfect! No deformities, no blemishes!'

'Dear Christ!'

They looked at each other, awed.

Alan led the way to the Rover.

# 18

Alan Charnock did not know what had happened, though he was aware of the change that had worked its way through him. From being physically in dread of his wife and the others corrupted by the ghoul from the Pit, he was now almost eager to confront them. He listened to the plans tumbling over and over in his mind in a half-admiring way. Amazingly, there were plans, realizable, well thought out plans. There was an excitement in conjecturing just how and when he and Ruane would intervene during the ritual. Alan was bewildered and delighted that he was no longer a trembling, complaisant coward.

He knew what to expect. There would be a moment of psychic imbalance. When it came, they must be ready, Ruane with the mystical power of the Cross and the Holy Water, he himself with the weapon most feared by evil.

Alan thought of the moment.

Just before the victim's heart was ripped open and the dark blood ran on the warm stone, that was the time. There would have been sexual depravity, and the invocation, maybe other forms of sacrifice. Then the frenzy of the women would stop. They would be paralysed. Janice might begin to jerk about in a silent spasm of agony, for she had to bear the weight of the grim Evil waiting beyond the dark on that night of so little darkness.

That was the moment, for the monster would be at its weakest

Alan felt his arms tensing. He could throw accurately, powerfully. The ex-priest sitting beside him noticed the slight movements.

Ruane recognized Alan's state of mind. The young man had eaten well, at his insistence, to restore his strength of body; but it was his mental resources that would be tested. In his condition, he would be uplifted by a vision of redemption for his young wife. He would see himself as a crusader, and for a while he would be buoyed up by his new-found confidence and self-esteem. But the exultation would not last. And what of himself? What of his own resilience?

Ruane felt for the slim silver flask of Holy Water and the smooth crucifix. There was the other weight too, the one he had not mentioned to the young man. He hoped he would not need it. Doubt ate into his mind. Had they made a mistake in tackling the monster without help?

He was beginning to regret his decision. The matter should have been reported to the authorities. It was not possible that the poor possessed women would attempt a sacrifice such as had been described to him in the lonely white-painted hospital room in the old abbey. No. They were not savages. They were educated and civilized women. The theft of a spastic child had been a coincidence.

All evening he and Charnock had listened to the news broadcasts. There were no reports of babies stolen, no mention of youngsters straying from home. No. It was not possible.

Just the same, Ruane regretted not telling the police of the matter. At least they would stop the horrible business, at Scinlaw.

Then Ruane remembered his own dealings with the police at the time of his arrest. They had been courteous at first, but not for long. His humiliation had been finely drawn out over months of investigation. Their brutal laughter echoed in his mind for years.

If he brought them out to the moors to see an apparently harmless if silly midnight ritual, they would jeer at him. And they would check to see if he had a record as a voyeur. And find enough to confirm them in their contempt.

And if the ritual was stopped, what then?

Janice Charnock would still be possessed. The evil spirit within her would clamour for life and, finding none, it would strike out in its rage. It would rend her apart. Ruane licked his lips. The memory of his flayed nerves made his flesh crawl. To calm himself, he talked to

Alan Charnock as the Rover sped through the darkening lanes:

'You'll see things you'll hardly be able to watch, Alan. Can you keep quiet? It isn't a normal exorcism — I can't be sure that any part of the ritual will conform to what I've been led to expect. It's an unknown force, completely unknown!'

'You'll manage.'

'There isn't any identifiable form for this kind of Evil! It's just a mindless force that has no affinity with finite life, but which nevertheless can take over a human soul and live some kind of tormented existence. It's a husk — a shell left over from Creation. But it has terrible force . . . It reeks of evil! I could smell its stench.'

Ruane admitted his fears to himself.

After a while, Alan said: 'At the séance, there were different stenches. Musk was one. The others I don't know. Something like garlic, but not quite.'

'Asafoetida,' said Ruane. 'One of the signs of an evil presence. Musk too.'

'You told this priest you went to see?'

Ruane watched the last of the hazy

217

afterglow settling on the rearing rock-edges. He felt sick with apprehension, he could feel nerves twitching all over his body. He had made a solemn promise, but only to himself. One drink would not harm. But not until Alan Charnock couldn't see him.

'Did this priest — this monk — say anything about it?' repeated Alan.

Ruane thought of the thin face of the man who had written to him, reaching out to his misery with a few words of forgiveness. And of the stories he had told.

'I described the Evil just as you experienced it. The stench, the rotting stuff from the grave. The blood. The power. He knew of a similar phenomenon. It was at the time when the Belgians left Africa. A ghoul was loose, without intelligence, its only reason for existence to inflict evil. There was a blood-bath. He was there, and he says he was sure that some terrible Presence was loose in the land. The Africans knew it too. Wherever it went, there was blood, rivers of blood.'

'And?'

'There was no effective government, so the tribal elders took their spears and tracked it down. A band of guerrillas had captured a village. It was there amongst them, powerful and ravening,' Ruane said. 'No one knew which particular person it had infected, or whether it was the whole band. The spears couldn't tell the difference, and the fire rained into the huts destroyed all.'

There was silence for some minutes. Alan Charnock let the Rover take the narrow bends slower now. He felt freer than he had ever been. He could make up his mind without referring to anyone else. Janice had always decided domestic matters, Jerry Hood had been the one who made decisions in the office. All his adult life, Alan realized, he had depended on the judgment of others.

Even now, he could not manage without an adviser. Nevertheless, there were some things he could do. The fire-bombs, for instance. Ruane had wanted something less lethal, but he hadn't seen the thing. Ruane knew it only from the medium's lips, as she recalled what it had said to Janice. If there was to be fire, then let it be furious!

He switched off the headlights a mile from the escarpment. He was cautious now. At the spot he had selected earlier, he eased the Rover across the coarse grass towards the shadow of the looming rock. Alan reversed the car, so that it faced towards the road. He pointed to the ridge.

'Up there. It takes a few minutes, then we can see across to the rock circle.'

He took a briefcase from the boot. Ruane looked up at the raw edges of the escarpment and was suddenly cold. There didn't seem to be much to say.

'I'll lead,' Alan told him.

Ruane waited until he was a few paces ahead.

The darkness hid his furtive movements and though Ruane's hands trembled, he held the whisky bottle with a drunkard's infinite care. Alan Charnock did not hear the soft gurgling.

'*Just this one!*' Ruane said to himself, hoping he did not lie. A slow warmth trickled through his body. 'One more.' He drank again. Charnock turned but Ruane had the bottle out of sight:

'Their cars,' Alan said, pointing.

They had found a track, concealed from the road. Clever, thought Alan, with the insidious cunning of night-beasts. They would not be disturbed if any forethought on their part could prevent it.

The afterglow had gone, but the sliver of moon gave some light. Against the rocks and heather, and the tufts of coarse grass, the tracks were easy to follow, worn by the sharp feet of sheep since the thrifty Benedictines brought them to the wet wildernesses of the Pennines. In the gloom ahead, the circle of stones sat like a monstrous cyst on the dark moorland.

Ruane cursed as he tripped in a marshy hollow.

'Quiet,' hissed Alan.

They were a hundred yards away, and sound carried freely in the clear air. But from the black circle of Scinlaw, nothing.

Ruane had twisted his ankle. 'Give me a moment,' he said.

Alan Charnock checked his pockets for

the hundreth time. Matches. A lighter. The wads of cotton wool. He shivered as he thought of Janice and the women amongst the great rocks. There was no sound, no hint of life.

He wondered if they too were waiting. 'I'll get closer,' he said. 'You wait.'

'No! Not yet! Watch!'

Ruane felt his assurance returning. After all, he had not needed much whisky. It had invigorated him. He thought of passing the bottle to Charnock. No. He wouldn't understand Ruane's need, nor did he need the flaring solace of alcohol, not in his state of exaltation.

He peered into the darkness. 'What's the time?' he said.

'Half past eleven.'

'Soon,' said Ruane.

Far away, a night-owl sent out its warning cry. The moon glittered harshly, and the fat stars had a golden brilliance rarely seen in England. Alan Charnock let his hands rest on a rock. He had known it would be warm.

Minutes passed slowly, and gradually Alan began to question his belief in himself. He looked down for the briefcase and could not see it. Panicking, he scrabbled in the heather and found it at once. He opened it carefully, noiselessly.

'Anything wrong?' whispered Ruane, still peering into the moon washed circle.

'No.'

It was so silent that he could hear the ticking of his watch. He looked. Twenty minutes to twelve.

Ruane blinked hard. The moonlight was fading.

Alan sensed the diminishing of the light too. Both men looked at each other, and then at the sliver of moon.

'A blood moon,' he said.

The sickle was edged with a red glow.

Ruane examined it for a moment. 'It's an atmospheric thing. I've heard of it.' He stopped, because the circle of stones was suddenly alive with light. Yellow and green flames came from five points, equidistant about the too-regular black slab.

'Christ,' breathed Alan.

'It's begun,' said Ruane. He could see Charnock's thin features in the strange, unearthly light. 'Remember. It's only the beginning. Remember!'

*Worse*, Ruane had said. How much worse would it be?

'Yes.'

'It's only flame. Sulphur and something else. They've done it in the traditional way.'

'They would,' said Alan. 'They would.'

'Give them a few minutes, then we'll get nearer,' said Ruane.

'They'll hear us coming.'

'No.' Ruane wished he could share the bottle. 'They'll have things to occupy them. And you must not let them know we're here — don't call out! *Remember*!'

At that moment, Alan heard a great shout from a dozen eldritch voices:

'Kelipoth! Kelipoth!'

Cold sweat sprang out on Alan's neck. He felt the tightening of the scalp that brought the hair on his neck upright. Ruane breathed a prayer.

It had begun.

Both men watched, unable to blink, so hard was their concentration.

There was silence for perhaps two

seconds, and then Janice's high voice rang out:

'Kelipoth no more, my King!'

Then from amongst the rocks, women ran out into the brightly-lit centre. At a distance of a hundred yards, the figures were just identifiable. Black shadows leapt, faces showed green and yellow, arms windmilled, legs flashed. Someone screamed with the sheer evil joy of it all.

'Myra,' said Alan.

She stood still for a moment, and he saw her mouth wide open, holding that triumphant, screaming yell as it bounced from rock to rock and sank away into the darkness of the moors.

Janice, slim and white, hair a silver shawl around her thin shoulders, advanced on her. She was naked, and her body was alive with cabbalistic markings.

'Be still,' Ruane said in a low and controlled voice. 'For her life, be still!'

# 19

Alan watched it in a kind of horrified delirium.

The women — the terrible women! — scrabbled at one another like beasts. They tore and flung away their clothes in an ecstasy of delight. Janice moved wraith-like, a slim white priestess of evil, and then the frenzy gripped them.

Aghast, Alan watched the writhing, grunting couplings. It was sick and unreal.

The only thing that mattered, though, was Janice's abstention from the debased, perverted rites. She laughed, she yelled approval, she wandered from pair to pair, but she took no active part in the happenings.

Then Alan realized that hers was the most debased part all, for it was Janice who urged on the willing worshippers.

The Baines-Ogden woman howled like a mad dog. A beautiful dark-haired girl ran to her, sobbing with delight. Two older women staggered about short-sightedly, fumbling a new partner. Their heavy bodies gleamed with sweat, yellow and green, shining as if oiled.

'Ruane — '

'Not yet.'

Ruane drank again as Alan stared, hypnotized, at the circle.

There was some kind of signal from Janice. Slowly, the women parted. Janice spoke to them softly.

'Closer now,' breathed Ruane. 'Careful.'

'But — '

'They're unaware of anything but themselves. And what they do.'

It was true. The women formed a somnambulistic group about the grim black slab where the flames guttered and black smoke drifted. They were in a trance. An ecstatic abandonment had dulled their senses. They were drunk with lust, trembling with an unholy air of expectation as they listened to Janice.

'All right,' Alan said, gulping down the nausea he felt. 'Now.'

Alan led, keeping to the shelter of the rocks. The handle of the briefcase was sticky in his hand. The back of his sack felt clammy. He shook as he thought of the great evil shape.

Behind him Ruane drank with secret skill. He stumbled, keeping the bulk of his body-weight on his sound ankle. The moon was a duller red, its poor light making progress difficult. Yet, a comforting haze began to settle inside him, rising softly to his head. The whisky had done its work. He wondered if he had drunk too much. No. Exactly the right amount to restore his confidence whilst leaving his faculties unimpaired. It had been a foolish promise, quite right that he had disregarded it.

Janice's voice rose. The two men stopped. There was an unmistakable command in her voice. The women rushed to obey, bare feet slapping on grass and worn soil.

From thirty yards away, Alan and Ruane watched, hidden in the deep shadow of a toad-shaped rock.

A small woman brought long peeled

wands. Others took them and set them in the ground about the low rectangular slab. Ruane pointed:

'A pentagon. See.'

Encompassing the black rock and outlined, in a whitish paint or powder, was the five-starred shape Alan had seen at the medium's house. A wand now dipped at each point.

'What are they — '

'Quiet!'

There was little need for them to whisper, for all the women were occupied. Five of them, smiling horribly, deposited wicker baskets beside each long dipping white wand.

'Cypress boughs,' said Ruane to stop the young man's questions. 'The circle is the emblem of death, and cypress of the graveyard.'

Satisfied with the position of the baskets, Janice called to them, in a voice again too low for the men to hear. The women stepped inside the pentagon and waited. She looked all about at their patient, evil-smiling faces.

'*You must not move!*' Alan heard, and

for a moment a spasm shook his body. Then he realized that it was Ruane warning him once more not to intervene. ''No matter what — remember!'

Janice pointed to the Baines-Ogden woman.

Alan remembered the woman's bitter fury when her lost dog was found, torn in an earlier bloody sacrifice. She had the look now of a sinner promised eternal happiness. Her face was radiant.

Low murmurs of congratulation came from the circle of women, and then fluting, eager laughter from the chosen one.

She walked to one of the baskets.

A growling, sobbing, spitting came from the basket as the woman wrenched back the lid. Alan thought of a baby missing, of white faces against a shop-front, of the careful and wary look of the policemen when they asked where he had spent the night.

He shook with relief when the Baines-Ogden woman held up her prize.

It was a cat.

All the women watched. Janice nodded.

Alan saw the red sickle of a moon behind her, and somewhere within the pentagon, a hint of a gathering evil.

Ruane had him firm when he tried to move to save the terrified creature. Alan sobbed, but he was still. The cat died. Raking claws meant nothing to the woman. Her big hands held it by body and head, and with one easy wrench she broke its neck.

Janice murmured in appreciation, and touched a slim girl with her hand. The slim girl ran, giggling with delight, to take the limp body. In seconds, she had looped it to the swaying wand.

'Don't watch,' Ruane breathed.

Alan smelt the whisky, but he was too far gone into a private and horrific world to care. The Baines-Ogden woman was already breaking the neck of a second cat.

'Get ready,' Ruane said thickly. 'Here!'

He pushed the briefcase at Alan.

Now, Alan could identify the fumes.

'Whisky?' he said, very quietly. He felt cold, cold and alone.

'Quiet.'

Alan held the briefcase, hands slipping

on its greasy handle. More cats spat and howled, then died, to dangle like macabre fruit.

Janice moved again, very slowly, her white body aglow and alive with the symbolic markings Alan had seen before. They matched the thin muscles, the angular shape of hip and thigh, the delicate dipping curves of her breasts. And they made patterns of their own, a series of images; their intent was plain: they called to evil.

The women held their stations, and the two men could see that they were very tense now. On the Baines-Ogden woman's shoulders, the heavy muscles stood out like those of a wrestler attempting a fall. A faint, sly sound came from them, weird and low.

'The invocation!' Ruane muttered. 'Dear Christ, if Thou art near, give us Thy comfort and strength in the trial that is to come!'

The keening, sighing sound came from almost closed lips. In unison, the women began a chant. Flaring suddenly, the sulphur torches gobbeted fire and smoke straight up into the still air.

Janice made a sign. The sound ceased. She turned until she was facing the north. Her slim arms came up with a wonderfully graceful movement. Alan saw her begin that tender, brilliant smile.

'Come?'

The word was like the peal of a silver bell.

It had a world of longing in it.

She waited, the others too. Alan and Ruane held their breath, aware that the intent circle of naked women were waiting with an ecstatic excitement.

For a moment, the sulphur flames sank. The warm night air sank into the ground. A thin mist began to edge over the great black slabs.

'My King?'

Janice's voice rang out, sweet as honey, cold as ice.

Ruane saw the knife in her hand. He pressed his bulk against Charnock's wide thin shoulders, pinning him:

'No,' he muttered.

Janice's hand came up, and the steel glittered dully.

'Come?' she said.

Alan watched as his wife drew the knife down her body. Blood trickled, grey-red and heavy, onto the slab. He could not move. He noticed Ruane's stinking breath and felt a spurt of fury. But he said nothing.

Janice shrieked into the sky, a formless word.

The chill was worse. Blood drained from her.

For a moment, a gathering something hovered over the grim black slab. A lost, iron-edged grating sound came from it, as if from a million miles beyond the Universe.

Janice screamed again, a tormented, desperate shriek.

Then the lights burned stronger, and the night was warm again. The women knew they had failed. They fell to their knees, echoing Janice's wild shrieks.

'Now?' whispered Alan.

'*No!*'

'You're afraid! You're drunk!' Alan snarled, fury rising again. But his voice was low and secret. 'You've brought whisky, you drunken bastard!'

'For your wife's sake — if you ever wish to see her whole again — be *silent*!'

Alan opened the briefcase and felt for the small glass containers. Still watching the grim circle, he prepared methodically.

He could no longer think rationally.

'One last sacrifice,' said Ruane heavily. 'It is time.'

Alan barely heard him. He had relied on Ruane, and the ex-priest had shown himself to be a drunken sot. But that did not matter, for Alan could decide when to act. He could not reason now. He had the strength of his will and of his body, but his intellectual resources were battered into fragments.

He knew only that, when the moment came, he would act.

He saw Janice point to the beautiful dark-haired girl, but he did not recognize her. The thought brought almost a wry smile, for recognition was not easy, not when the women were naked maniacs.

'Blood!' called Janice, and she spoke with the iron in her voice Alan remembered from that earlier ghastly manifestation at Mrs. Worrall's.

The dark-haired girl froze.

Janice burst into a wild invocation, thick with the names of demons. Moaning sighs accompanied her impassioned chanting.

Her despair evoked in Alan a poignant sense of loss. Such a power of love and longing, and all aimed at the Evil thing that had almost taken on life.

He had the matches ready, and he knew exactly where Ruane had placed the silver flask of Holy Water. Two elements, fire and water, to destroy the insubstantial monster.

Minutes slid away.

The moon reddened.

'Bring it!' screamed Janice suddenly.

The Baines-Ogden woman leapt to answer her signal.

She was out of the pentagon for a few seconds only. When she returned, she carried a box-like shape.

'Dear Christ, no,' breathed Alan.

It was a baby's carrying-basket.

The dark-haired girl shrieked when she saw it.

'It's a child — ' began Alan.

'Not yet,' growled Ruane.

'Yes!' snarled Alan aloud, and Ruane looked up sharply. The women had not heard. Three of them held the shrieking girl.

'It must be a life for a life!' screamed Janice to her. 'Blood for my king!'

The dark-haired girl opened her mouth wide again. But the others had fixed her with the terrible basilisk glare. Her knees buckled.

Then she nodded weakly.

'Blood,' she said. Then, more strongly: 'Blood for the King!'

'Ruane,' grated Alan. 'It's her own child!'

'And we'll stop them — but just a few seconds longer! When the Evil thing is nearer — when it forms! And then it can be destroyed forever!'

The sacrifice was quickly prepared. A bubbling noise came from the cot, and then a tiny form was held up in the flaring light.

Myra Bentley looked closely at the plump limbs:

'Perfect!' she howled.

Janice smiled.

Tenderly the Baines-Ogden woman laid the tiny form on the black rock. It looked up at her and let out a single mew of complaint.

The yellow lights dimmed. In a matter of two or three seconds a freezing fog sprang up, thicker, stronger than before.

Ruane fumbled with the cap of the silver flask. Alan felt his whole body alive with a tremendous power.

But when the Shape spangled the northern point of the pentacle with a ghastly blue-white iridescence, both men were paralysed.

It was gross, formless, but with such an evil, writhing symmetry and a grotesque, rearing deadliness that they were stilled by the terror it struck through and through their flesh and bones.

Janice howled with joy:

'My King!'

The women abased themselves, rolling their hair in the thick grass.

The monstrous shape emitted sounds. Broken iron-edged gutturals clanged about the black rocks.

Janice seemed to understand.

'Yes! Yes! Oh yes!' She raised the knife.

Alan put a match to sandpaper.

A tiny light flickered.

The freezing fog at once extinguished it.

'Christ!' Alan burst out

He looked up: 'Janice! For God's sake, darling, don't do it — if you ever loved me, just don't do it!'

There was a long, frozen silence.

'I'll move — ' Ruane said, at last removing the top of the flask. He stumbled forward.

Janice turned in the direction of the interruption. Her eyes were red wheels in the dimness of the almost-extinguished sulphur flares.

Alan looked away, but Ruane caught the full blast of that terrible stare. He was again paralysed.

Alan was quite calm.

He readied the lighter. Its long flame would be better than matches. One bottle in each coat pocket, cotton wool already soaked.

He kicked Ruane out of his way and took the silver flask from his slack hand.

'Wait!' groaned Ruane, seizing the crucifix tight. 'Alan, let me — '

He put his weight on the torn ligaments of his ankle and cried out in pain. But he fought it and followed, the crucifix upraised.

Alan was at the edge of the circle.

The monstrous Shape was silent, tense, waiting, vulnerable, neither part of this world nor a shadowy wanderer of the Abyss.

Alan could have laughed.

The baby waved its hands to him as he strode through the ring of naked bodies. Not one of the women looked up. They sweated, streaked with dirt and black soot, in attitudes of complete abasement.

'Janice!' roared Alan.

The eyes spun, but he had acted.

He let the clear stream of Holy Water wash over the grim sacrificial altar. The baby saw the drops and reached for them.

Then he threw the silver flask at Janice.

It caught her neck and the water splashed her sweating body. She shrieked, and in that moment Alan saw the flesh burn.

He was in a frenzy himself by now.

He saw that Ruane had staggered after him, but did not care, nor did he care when the women lifted their heads.

The crucifix held high, Ruane hobbled after him.

Then the women slowly blocked his path, and he could not reach Alan.

Ruane felt their eyes on him, and pure terror filled his soul. Suddenly the crucifix was too heavy and he had to let it sink. Then it was a glowing brand, shot through with white fire.

He let it drop.

With the terror of death came a knowledge that he had failed the man who trusted him. Yet he could not pass those terrible women, he could not take one step further.

The Evil had won. He was resigned to it.

And then, suddenly and without warning, the women were rushing away from him and he could see their panic and terror, see it and hear it as Janice screamed again and again to the rearing monstrous Shape:

'My King, my King!'

A dull, flat explosion rocked her.

Ruane saw what caused it.

Alan Charnock had thrown a petrol-bomb clear into the middle of the terrible Presence's wraith-like outline,

Fire boiled, licking at the chill, coiled Evil.

Then Alan Charnock lit the second bomb and hurled it straight and true. The explosion was louder.

The screaming of the women increased, and in it was an outraged fury, a threatening and terrifying violence. Ruane gasped and staggered forward.

The great Shape was already fading. Heat surged towards the black slab, and the baby cried its wonderment at the flames.

Janice watched blindly.

Then Alan Charnock turned away from his new-made inferno and sought his wife.

Ruane knew what would happen.

Alan was transfigured. The haggard

features were sharp and bold. He was an avenging archangel.

'Look away!' bawled Ruane at the top of his lungs. 'For God's sake, man, *look away!*'

All the women faced the young man. He was too far gone into his ecstasy to know. He called to Janice:

'It's over! It's gone! Janice, I love you!'

She sighed, a snake's deadly whisper:

'*Kelipoth!*'

The women were one with Janice, all eyes fixed.

Alan caught their concentrated, shaft-like stare.

He raised his arms to Janice and slowly sank to the ground, eyes open, mouth calling silently even as he fell.

Ruane ran, pushing naked bodies aside.

He put a hand to the thin chest. Alan Charnock was dead.

\* \* \*

In the next half-hour or so, the women came out of their trance. They dressed when they saw their own nakedness. They seemed to know what they had done. The beautiful dark-haired girl caressed the baby in an amazed torment. Janice stayed by Alan, apparently emotionless. Ruane found a small electric lamp and buried the dead animals.

He waited, with the sure knowledge that shame and fear would follow. He could deal with the aftermath of disaster where he could not avert it.

'Go home,' he told the women.

At last, Janice came to him.

'Alan's dead,' she said.

'I'll stay with him.'

She shook with pain. 'Why did we do it?' she asked. The thing had left her.

'God knows,' said Ruane.

'I'm burned!' she sobbed. 'And cut.'

'Not deeply. The burn-marks will pass. It's a mental thing, not real. Go home.'

The other women filtered away into the darkness.

'Can I wait too?'

'Call for an ambulance, then come back.'

'I loved Alan.'

'He knew it.'

'The police — '

'No police,' said Ruane.

'But Alan's dead! We — we — '

'You did nothing. Keep to that. His heart failed. There will be no investigation.'

There had been enough evil that night. Ruane thought of the endless questioning, the wary eyes, the certainty of life-long suspicion, and the broken homes.

'No police!' said Ruane again.

The night was almost gone when the ambulance came.

The men arranged the long, slim body with care, but when he saw it, Ruane was not satisfied.

'May I?' he asked.

They looked at the scarred, worn symbol. 'Yes, sir.'

Ruane laid the crucifix between Alan's hands.

They took him away as the first tinge of pink brought the dawn.

'I loved him!' Janice sobbed. 'I did.'

Ruane began the long gentle process of restoring her peace of mind. And, at last, his skilled compassionate words allowed her to face the day.

Ruane wondered how he himself would face the days, always the accusing tomorrows. He let the remains of the whisky dribble onto the blackened grass.

There was a letter to write, a report. It had been demanded of him. And he would say that he had betrayed a trust once more.

★　★　★

There was yet to be some consolation for Ruane.

A month later, he was summoned. The man who lay in the monastery hospital bed was racked by spasms of pain, yet he radiated an air of hope and absolute confidence.

He didn't want Ruane to say much

'I read your letter,' he whispered, and his words had the quiet rustling sound of paper blown across grass. 'You think you failed?'

'Yes.'

'No!' the man said, and his voice was

stern. 'The young man died, but would he have wanted it any other way? He had to save the child, and he had to try to keep the Evil thing from his young wife! Because you stumbled and apparently failed him, you blame yourself — and there is no blame attaching to you, none. Not the shadow of a hint of blame.'

Ruane would have interrupted, but a slight gesture stilled him.

'Within every person, there is a core of truth, the part that remains when all the rest is stripped away. When conceit and pride and self-esteem go, and position and power and authority with them, then the true man is revealed. You were stripped, layer by layer, when you lost your vocation, and you had to find yourself again, build up from that naked core. You were reborn, Ruane! In seeking out the demon as you did, you took the first step to a new kind of existence. You began to put together a new man, Ruane, and if you only forgive yourself for this seeming failure, then you will be a finer man than you once were — than when you had the care of souls!'

247

The voice was fading.

A young lay-brother filled a syringe,

'No, my son,' said the dying man. 'Not that. Not with drug-soaked visions.'

The young man bowed.

'Ruane?' said the rustling voice.

'Here, Father.' Ruane watched, panic rising inside him.

'You know what you must do to achieve a full rehabilitation?'

'To get back into the ministry?'

There was anger again on the emaciated face.

'That way is barred to you,' he whispered harshly. 'Accept it and take the other path.'

Ruane could see the drawn, anguished face of Alan Charnock for a moment. And then the fire, boiling and roaring, and the monstrous Shape roaring its terror to the ends of the Universe.

'You have a gift!' the dying man said, his voice strong at last. 'Use it! Seek out the Adversary and utterly confound Him! God knows there are few enough today who dare confront the Devil when He rides out! Ruane, you'll not fail — you have a gift, and it is your God-given duty to use it.'

Ruane took the proffered hand, thin and dry and hot, in his own. It was a valediction.

'Please?' said the lay-brother.

'I won't fail,' Ruane said sombrely.

'Pray God you won't. Pray now!'

Ruane knelt at the bedside and did not notice the arrival of the small procession. Nor did he hear the solemn intoning of the last rites.

An hour passed and he looked up. He knew then that he had no friend in the world, only a grim and inevitable duty.

It had been put on him.

He would bear it.

### THE END

We do hope that you have enjoyed reading this large print book.

Did you know that all of our titles are available for purchase?

We publish a wide range of high quality large print books including:
**Romances, Mysteries, Classics**
**General Fiction**
**Non Fiction and Westerns**

Special interest titles available in large print are:
**The Little Oxford Dictionary**
**Music Book, Song Book**
**Hymn Book, Service Book**

Also available from us courtesy of Oxford University Press:
**Young Readers' Dictionary**
**(large print edition)**
**Young Readers' Thesaurus**
**(large print edition)**

For further information or a free brochure, please contact us at:
**Ulverscroft Large Print Books Ltd.**
**The Green, Bradgate Road, Anstey**
**Leicester, LE7 7FU, England.**
**Tel:** (00 44) **0116 236 4325**
**Fax:** (00 44) **0116 234 0205**